Browsing

The front door to the book store was propped open to let in the warm, sweet summer breeze, so Sasha didn't hear the bell that usually alerted her to a customer's entrance. Instead she was aware she was no longer alone in the store when a movement a few aisles away caught her eye. She looked up.

It was a boy, or rather a young man. He definitely looked older than the Kennedy crowd. He was tall and tanned, and his sandy hair was a little bit long and curly around his neck. He was wearing cutoff jeans and a faded orange T-shirt. And though he was wearing glasses, they couldn't hide the brightness of his hazel eyes.

Sasha caught his eye and smiled inquiringly, but he just smiled back and started working his way around the stacks until he reached the history section. Sasha left him alone — browsers were always welcome at the Albatross. She looked back down at her book. She'd read just one more page . . . okay, she'd finish the chapter. Sasha jumped. The sandy-haired boy was standing in front of her, his bright hazel eyes smiling down at her.

"Do you need some help?" she asked.

Books from Scholastic
in the Couples series:

Coming Soon . . .

Couples Special Edition
Summer Heat!

CHANGING PARTNERS

by M.E. Cooper

SCHOLASTIC INC.
New York Toronto London Auckland Sydney

No part of this publication may be reproduced in whole or in part, or stored in a retrieval system, or transmitted in any form or by any means, electronic, mechanical, photocopying, recording, or otherwise, without written permission of the publisher. For information regarding permission, write to Scholastic Inc., 730 Broadway, New York, NY 10003.

ISBN 0-590-40235-8

Copyright © 1986 by Cloverdale Press. All rights reserved. Published by Scholastic Inc.

12 11 10 9 8 7 6 5 4 3 2 1   6   6 7 8 9/8 0 1/9

Printed in the U.S.A.   06

Chapter
1

"Good-bye, dears. Have a good time! Drive safely, okay?" Sasha Jenkins grinned at her mom and dad as she struck a parental pose.

"You're sure you don't mind being cooped up in the bookstore all day?" her father asked, mussing Sasha's long dark hair. "School's out, the sun is shining, all your buddies are probably at the pool, in the park. . . . We don't *have* to — "

"Go!" Sasha commanded firmly, pointing to the station wagon. "Just don't forget to come back!"

She waved them off, standing on the front step. When the old blue station wagon had disappeared from view, she flung her arms wide exuberantly. Junior year at Kennedy High in Rose Hill, Maryland, was history! And this was going to be the best summer of her life.

She performed a quick pirouette, her arms still held wide, dark hair flying. How could her summer be anything but fantastic? First, there was

1

Wes. They were in love, with the prospect of countless romantic summer nights before them. And if that wasn't enough, she had a summer job at her parents' bookstore, the Albatross.

The chance to read — to gobble up every volume in the store — who could call that work? She'd still have time to spend outdoors and with her friends. Right now there was a new shipment of books to unpack — better than Christmas!

The phone rang before Sasha could pounce on the first carton. She picked it up, fully intending to say, "Good morning, this is the Albatross. May I help you?"

Instead, she found herself singing out, "Merry Christmas!" She clapped her hand over her mouth, but couldn't completely muffle the sound of her laughter.

"I must have the wrong number," murmured a baffled female voice on the other end of the line. By the time Sasha had collected herself enough to begin apologizing profusely, the caller had hung up. She shrugged — she might have just lost a customer, not exactly a good start to her first full day in charge of the store. But with any luck the woman would try again and nothing could shake her good mood today. "Merry Christmas — " Sasha giggled again.

She got down to work, first spreading out a copy of the order sheet on the counter. Now for the good part, actually opening the boxes.

The very first book she spotted was one by her favorite author, Edith Wharton. Sasha had read almost all the writer's books and loved them, but somehow she'd missed this one. She couldn't resist just glancing at the first page, then the second and third . . . she was hooked. She slid down to the floor, her back propped against the front of the counter, and began reading in earnest.

The front door to the Albatross was propped open to let in the warm, sweet summer breeze, so Sasha didn't hear the bell that usually alerted her to a customer's entrance. Instead she was aware she was no longer alone in the store when a movement a few aisles away caught her eye. She looked up.

It was a boy — or rather a young man. He definitely looked older than the Kennedy crowd. He was tall and tanned, and his sandy hair was a little bit long and curly around his neck. He was wearing cutoff jeans and a bright orange T-shirt.

Sasha caught his eye and smiled inquiringly, but he just smiled back and started working his way around the stacks until he reached the history section. Sasha left him alone — browsers were always welcome. She looked back down at her book. She'd read just one more page . . . okay, she'd finish the chapter. Sasha jumped. The sandy-haired boy was standing in front of her, his bright hazel eyes smiling down at her.

"Do you need some help?" she asked.

He squatted beside her and smiled. "If you're supposed to be unpacking these cartons, it looks like you're the one who could use some help. Let me give you a hand."

Sasha had closed *The House of Mirth*, and now he took the book gently from her hands. "Edith Wharton, hmm? She was really something else. It's a shame writers can't be immortal." It

3

was always nice to talk to somebody who felt the same way she did about books. Her friends tended to roll their eyes when she got started on her favorite author. "Yes, when I heard that she'd died, I thought about wearing black!"

"I know what you mean," he said. "When E.B. White died, we flew the flag at half-mast at my school."

She grinned. "You *did*? I grew up on *Charlotte's Web*. That sounds like a neat school."

"It is," he said, pushing a thick lock of hair back from his eyes. "I'm lucky to go to a college that offers so much."

Sasha felt a tingle at the base of her spine. She'd guessed he was older, but somehow the word *college* made her look at him anew. Still, he didn't make her feel shy; she leaned forward, her elbows on her knees, hoping he'd continue.

"I'm taking this fantastic seminar — you'd love it — just twenty students in the class. We're reading great books in the Western tradition, from the ancient Greeks — in Greek — to the twentieth century."

Sasha's eyes widened. "Greek?"

"Greek. I have to take two years of it. I'm also studying French." He dipped into the second carton and pulled out a volume. He sniffed it, laughing at Sasha's surprised expression. "A good book is like a fine wine, right?"

She joined his laughter, watching him run his fingers on the spine, their touch gentle, even reverent. He handled books the way she and her parents did, with affection and respect.

"Isaac Asimov. What a genius." He was sitting

4

next to her now, leaning against the counter only inches from her. He began to flip the pages.

"Granola bar?" Sasha offered, hospitably.

He took it with an absent nod of thanks, already lost in his reading.

Sasha turned back to her own book, but now she read with slightly less attention. She was very aware of the boy sitting next to her. A comfortable silence had filled the store, and she felt warm from the sun filtering through the plant-filled windows. She knew she should get to work unpacking the boxes but it was so tempting to sit here and daydream. . . .

Suddenly Sasha found herself being pulled to her feet and into Wesley Lewis's strong arms. Her book went flying and she shrieked with laughter as he twirled her around. She and Wes had been a couple for months now, but his touch was still magic to her, and she loved it when he greeted her with a hug and kiss to let the whole world know she belonged to him. Even though right now she felt just a little bit funny about making such a display in front of a stranger.

Wes retrieved the fallen book, glancing curiously at the boy sitting on the floor, and then turned to Sasha.

"Come on," he said, flashing her his dazzling smile, "pack up. We're going over to the cottage — my parents' summer place at Sherwood Forest. It's not far from Annapolis. Wait till you see it. There'll be sailing, a cookout — "

Sasha's face fell and Wes stopped in midsentence. "What's the matter, Sash?"

"I can't go with you, Wesley — I'm minding

5

the store today. Mom and Dad went to a book fair and left me in charge."

"Of course you can go," Wes contradicted her. "I told my parents we'd be there. My dad's home on leave — he's really counting on us."

Wesley's father was a career Navy man, and Wes was a student at Leesburg Academy, hoping someday to attend Annapolis and train to be a Navy pilot. Initially this interest had created big problems in their relationship — Sasha was a pacifist and a creative thinker and she'd had as hard a time understanding his goals as he had understanding her attitudes. But since that time they'd come to respect as well as love one another, despite their differences.

Now Sasha shrugged. She would be disappointed to miss a chance to spend the day with Wes and especially to meet Commander and Mrs. Lewis. Because Wes's father was on duty overseas so often, she had never had an opportunity to be introduced.

But she'd made a promise to her parents. "I have to unpack this shipment of books," Sasha told him, gesturing to the two large boxes by the counter.

Wes nodded, running a hand through his short dark hair. He appraised the situation, then set to work. He took all the books out of both cartons, stacked them on the counter, checked them off on the invoice, and sent Sasha off with a playful push to shelve them.

One book was still missing. Wes walked around the counter and peered at the title of the volume the boy in the orange T-shirt was reading.

"Would you like to purchase that, sir?" Wes asked in a firm, but polite tone.

"No, no thanks."

When Wes held his hand out for the book, the stranger gave it to him with a smile, and a wink — unobserved by Wesley — at Sasha. Wes made a final check of the invoice and handed the book to Sasha. She give it right back to the boy who'd been reading it.

"Hey, Sasha, don't you want to do this thing right?" Wes asked. Sasha heard the note of irritation in his voice — Wes was a stickler for proper procedure. And while she admired his seriousness — she was serious about the things she cared about, too — every now and then he needed someone to lighten him up.

"We're just that sort of bookstore," she said, teasingly. "This is a friendly place." Sasha took Wes by the hand and led him to the back of the store, where she put her arms around him and held him close.

"Hey, soldier, how about a dance?" His arms tightened around her and then his lips found hers in a slow, gentle kiss. Sasha rested her head on Wes's shoulders with a happy sigh; being with him always felt so right.

But her mind was still half on the store — she should really get back to the counter to keep an eye on things. She put her hands on his chest and pushed Wes a few inches away. He looked so handsome, with his crisp white polo shirt setting off his tanned, finely chiseled face.

Before she could speak, Wes asked, "Who is that guy, anyway?"

7

"I haven't the faintest idea," she answered. "Just one of your average book lovers."

"You looked like old friends, sitting on the floor together, eating granola bars. It's not the first time he's been here, is it?"

Sasha tilted her head and looked closely at him. There was something in his tone . . . it almost sounded as if he were jealous!

She wanted to tell him she thought he was adorable, but she didn't want to hurt his feelings. It wasn't often that Wes required assurance of her love. He was very accepting of the fact that she had a number of close male friends because he knew they didn't pose a romantic threat. But if he was feeling even the teensiest bit jealous now, she was happy to ease his mind. She reached up and kissed him lightly on the nose.

"Actually, this is his first time in the Albatross. He's a customer — I have to be civil to him."

"Some customer. He's not buying anything," snorted Wes, nuzzling her ear.

"You know my parents encourage everybody to come on in, have a cup of coffee, look around, talk about books and ideas. Sooner or later, almost everybody comes back to buy something." Sasha tried to keep her expression businesslike, but it was hard with Wes twirling a lock of her dark hair around his fingers, and melting her with that long-lashed gaze. It struck her now for the first time, though, that Wesley really didn't know a lot about the bookstore and the way it worked. Whenever he stopped in, it was to pick her up to go to a movie or the sub shop or a party, never just to hang around and talk.

A throat-clearing noise brought Sasha back down to earth. She pulled Wesley back around the corner to the front counter. It was the boy in the orange T-shirt. "Look, I'll be glad to mind the store for you until the boss comes back, if you could bring yourself to trust me."

The offer was surprising, but somehow Sasha felt as if she'd known him all her life — even if she didn't know his name! As if he'd read her mind, he spoke again. "I'm Rob Kendall."

"Wesley Lewis," Wes replied, holding out his right hand while putting his left arm firmly around Sasha's shoulders. "I suppose you know that this is Sasha Jenkins."

Rob's smile was extended to them both. "Sure, I've heard of your family. I'm house-sitting in Rose Hill for a while and the first stop in any new town is the bookstore, of course. Your parents are the owners, right?"

Sasha smiled broadly. "Yes, they are," she said. "Rob, that's a very nice offer, and I'm sure you'd be great at minding the store. But I think my parents might be a *little* surprised to find someone they've never met sitting behind the cash register when they get back."

"You're right," Rob said, returning her smile. "I get a little carried away in bookstores. I came in to check out what research material is available for the book I'm writing, and — "

"You're writing a book? You're an author?" Sasha interrupted him, clapping her hands together. "A real, live author right here in the Albatross?" She was the editor of the Kennedy High paper, *The Red and the Gold*, and hoped someday to be a journalist or novelist or playwright. But at present, she still felt funny describing herself as a *writer*. She had such a long way to go to attain true professional status.

Rob laughed and rolled his eyes. "I'm not published, yet. But I'm working on it."

"What is the book about?" Sasha inquired eagerly. "Is it fiction? Could I read your manuscript sometime, what you've finished so far?"

She couldn't help running on, she was so intrigued by Rob's confession, even though she knew Wes was getting impatient. He didn't have much to contribute to this kind of conversation. He still had his arm around her and she could feel his tension. But she wouldn't be rude and cut Rob off now, just as he was leaning against the counter, ready to launch into a description of his work.

Just then Kim Barrie burst into the Albatross, short brown hair flying, green eyes sparkling.

Kim and her mother ran a catering service called Earthly Delights, and now that school was out, Kim was working pretty much full-time. Right now, she was on the hunt for new and exciting cookbooks, she declared to Sasha, Wes, and Rob, who she shook hands with energetically.

She was full of enthusiasm. "Would you believe it? We're doing a party for Chan Lawrence, the tennis star! It's his nineteenth birthday. Is he ever one gorgeous hunk!"

Wes's eyebrows shot up. "I thought you were Woody's girl friend."

"That doesn't mean I can't appreciate a good-looking man," Kim said.

Wes looked from Kim to Sasha and back again. "Wouldn't you be upset if Woody drooled all over some other girl?" he asked.

"Probably not." Kim laughed. "What do you think, Sasha? We're women of the eighties, right? We might not want our guys paying too much attention to other girls, but *we* can certainly look now and then."

Sasha agreed with Kim, but today Wes seemed edgy and she didn't want to antagonize him, so instead of speaking right out in her usual way, she just smiled. She turned to Wes, hugging him around the waist.

"Why don't you go over to your parents' cottage and go sailing with your dad?" she prompted gently. "Maybe I can go next time."

Wes glanced over at Rob, as if he was reluctant to leave while the other boy was still in the store. Rob had been browsing in the history section; now he headed for the door.

"Have to go walk a dog," he said, grinning. "Not only am I house-sitting, I'm dog, cat, and goldfish sitting, too! I'll see you all around."

After he left, Kim said, "He's cute."

Sasha nodded. "He's writing a book. I never did find out what it's about, but I'll pin him down next time he comes in." He would be back, Sasha was sure of it.

Wes still had a possessive arm around Sasha and she thought she felt it tense again, just slightly. But when she looked into his eyes, all she could see was love and she knew her eyes were shining the same way. She must have imagined that he was jealous.

She walked out to the sidewalk with him, while Kim began studying titles in the cookbook section. The morning was heating up — it was going to be a beautiful summer day. Sasha took a deep, delicious breath.

"I'm sorry you can't come with me, Sasha," Wesley said. "But I understand how it is — you've made a commitment to your parents. I wouldn't want you to let them down."

It made Sasha happy to hear Wes say this; she'd worried for a moment he wouldn't understand why she wasn't free to go to Sherwood Forest when it was so important to him. She squeezed his hand.

"Thanks Wes, I'm sorry, too. I guess we just have to get used to a new routine. Instead of classes, meeting the gang for lunch on the quad, doing my homework, I have some other activities to juggle. But I'll have so much more time for you!" She gave him a quick hug.

"How about tonight, then — after you're finished with work?"

Sasha nodded, her eyes bright. "Tonight — that sounds wonderful." Wes kissed her good-bye, then moved off toward his car. Sasha watched him go, her heart nearly bursting with affection and pride. Wes was really one-of-a-kind. She knew she was lucky to date such a special guy. But now she had to put her mind back on the bookstore business. She ran back into the Albatross on tiptoe, to sneak up and scare Kim.

Chapter
2

Kim sailed through the streets of Rose Hill on her bicycle, whistling. It was a gorgeous day; the sun was shining and she could smell the honeysuckle that was in bloom all over town.

Of all the many places she had lived, this was the best, she decided. She waved at everybody she saw and everybody waved back. She belonged.

"Hi," she called out when she reached home and parked her bike up against the back porch.

She loved this renovated old house, more than all the other houses she and her family had ever lived in. And they'd lived in a number, moving every two years or so because her father, an advisor on Indian affairs with the Department of the Interior, kept getting transferred. This time around, he was based in D.C.

But this stop was different from the rest. Usually, by the time Kim managed to make a few real friends, it was time to pack up again. The kids at Kennedy High had gathered her into the crowd quickly, and it was a fantastic feeling to finally be a part of things.

Kim knew that crazy, adorable Woody Webster was more than a little responsible for her sense of belonging. He was everybody's friend. When he'd fallen in love with her, that had made her everybody's friend, too.

Rose Hill was really home to Kim now, and she hoped it would be home forever. Her family was putting down roots this time. They'd had a wonderful all-white high-tech kitchen installed so her mother could start a catering business, which was turning out to be an overwhelming success. And Kim knew her parents had made some new friends, too.

Kim, her mom's number one assistant, now followed her nose to find her boss. The nose told her that somebody, either a client or the family, was going to have a special supper — Mrs. Barrie's famous ragout.

Kim sniffed, analyzing the ingredients. No ordinary beef stew; it was cooked in red wine, with twelve spices and herbs, garden fresh vegetables, and served with homebaked French bread!

"I'm home," Kim announced, dropping her backpack on a chair. "Wait till you see the new cookbook — " She did a double-take. The figure at the counter was too tall to be Mrs. Barrie. The back was turned to her, but those red suspenders were a trademark, worn winter and summer, probably even with swim trunks, maybe even with pajamas.

14

"Hey, you're not my mother," she said, trying to keep a straight face.

Woody turned to give her a huge grin. "How did you guess?"

"My mother's hair is darker than yours, and it's not curly."

"Your mother had to run an errand. I told her I'd watch the stove for her."

"You're not watching, you're eating!" Kim feigned indignation. Woody guiltily relinquished the slice of French bread he'd just cut from a loaf that was cooling on a rack on the counter.

"I have no character," he admitted. "Can't resist French bread — or you."

He gathered her into his arms in a big, warm bear hug.

"If I had to choose, though, I guess I'd take you."

Kim giggled and Woody kissed her. "At least I think I would." He kissed her again and nodded. "Okay, I would, but we still have to keep our strength up." He picked her up and sat her on the counter, then buttered a second slice of bread.

Kim had no character either. "My mother wouldn't want me to starve," she said, biting into it with relish.

"Hey, Woody, you still haven't told me what you're doing here, besides sabotaging my mom's latest culinary creation. Why aren't you at the theater?" Woody's mother managed a small theater in Washington, D.C., called Arena Stage, and this summer he worked there part-time.

"It's Monday, space cadet, remember? We're closed today." Kim had dropped her flip flops to the floor and was swinging her bare feet; she aimed a light kick at Woody's stomach. He grabbed her foot and tickled its sole, then solemnly kissed her toes, while Kim shook with laughter.

"Besides, I primarily stopped by with a business proposition. Young lady, please be serious. Tell me this isn't the best idea you've ever heard — you and your talented mom could open the Stage Door Deli, right next to my theater!"

Kim made a face.

"It would be a winner," Woody insisted. "Run an exhaust pipe outside and the gorgeous aromas from the Barrie cooking would pack 'em in."

"People from miles around would storm the deli," Kim grinned wickedly. "Nobody would go to the theater. You and your mother would go broke. We'd have to feed you, out of the goodness of our hearts, to keep you out of the gutter. You'd eat up all of the profits. You're already eating up all the profits!" She slapped Woody's hand, which was reaching for another piece of bread.

"The door from the street would be one way — in. To leave, the diners would have to go through another door, into the theater."

"You must be hard up for customers," she teased.

"*Au contraire!* We're packed to the rafters. Okay, turn that around. We'll have the exit from the theater lead into your deli."

Kim knew Woody was kidding, but she also knew that he would love to have her working next to him so they would be together every day, as well as spending time on the weekends and dates at night. She knew she didn't have to remind him that she needed — they *both* needed — space, and time alone to do their own things.

Woody had almost lost her once, by sticking too close and being too serious. She loved being part of the gang and half of a couple as much as he did, but that just wasn't all there was to life in Kim's view. Although, right now she was happier than she'd ever been, and it was all too tempting to let Woody tuck her in his pocket and keep her safe forever.

Kim continued pretending to scoff and Woody acknowledged defeat.

"Okay, then," he said cheerfully. "No Stage Door Deli. Instead, we'll hire a chemist to synthesize the aromas from the kitchen. Bottle it as a perfume. A little dab behind the ear and a person will be irresistible. No kidding! We'll corner the market. Say yes to this scheme or I'll have to drown my sorrows in ragout."

"You nut!" Kim hopped off the counter to give him an adoring hug.

Mrs. Barrie arrived just then, carrying an overflowing grocery bag. Woody took it from her and began unpacking it. Kim's mother shook her head in mock dismay when she saw the remnants of of the French bread. She took the cover off the crock pot and checked the stew.

"I was thinking of inviting you to dinner tonight, Woody," she said dryly, with a warm smile in her daughter's direction.

"Thanks Mrs. B.," said Woody blithely, "but I've already eaten your dinner."

Kim snapped him with a dish towel.

"I said I'd watch the stove," Woody said innocently. "I did. I watched the French bread. It began to disappear. I watched the crock pot — the ragout began to disappear, too. I'll write it all up in my report."

"I guess that's fair exchange for the use of your car, dear," Mrs. Barrie said, handing him back the keys to his Volvo.

That explained the mystery of how Woody had arrived without leaving any evidence outside, either car or bike. "And all the time I thought you'd borrowed a broomstick," Kim mused. "What happened to your car, Mom?"

"It's in the little red wagon hospital," Mrs. Barrie told her daughter. "Woody was kind enough to lend me his wheels.

"Don't go yet, Woody," Mrs. Barrie added, as if Woody had the slightest intention of leaving. "I want some input on a menu for the party at the Lawrences."

"Woody can't cook!" Kim reminded her.

"No, but I can eat," he responded. "I'm a champion in that field, highly qualified to help with a menu. Right up my alley."

"I'm torn," Mrs. Barrie confessed. "The options are limitless. We could have an elaborate buffet with roast beef, hot Parker House rolls, scalloped potatoes, tossed salad. Or. . . ."

Woody rubbed his hands together with a devious grin. "I'd be more than happy to put on a white coat and chef's hat and stand behind the serving table to slice the meat, Mrs. Barrie," he offered.

"You'd eat the whole thing!" Kim giggled.

"How about a fish fry?" Mrs. Barrie made another suggestion.

"When? Where?" came a voice from the front hall. "We'd be happy to come. What should I bring? How about a nice cold watermelon?"

There was no mistaking that husky voice. It belonged to Brenda Austin, along with the big brown eyes and beautiful smile that now peeked around the doorway into the kitchen.

"I'm just kidding, Mrs. Barrie. Hi, you guys. Brad and I are on our way to the sub shop — is anybody interested?"

Brad was right beside her, his arm casually but firmly draped across her shoulders. It occurred to Kim that Brad must have gotten the afternoon off from the hospital where he was working as an orderly. He put in long hours; she knew that both he and Brenda looked on what time they did have to spend together as incredibly precious. With Brad leaving for Princeton in the fall, it was especially important for them to make the most of summer vacation.

As usual Brenda looked great, in straight, red-and-white-striped cigarette-leg trousers, and an oversized white T-shirt. Kim couldn't help admiring the attractive contrast she made to Brad, dressed in classic Bermuda shorts and an Oxford-cloth shirt. She and Woody were certainly a different sort of pair! Kim's fashion priority was comfort and Woody's taste in clothing could only be described as eclectic.

"Mrs. Barrie," Brad said seriously, "why don't you run a cooking school? Teach Brenda to cook

19

like that. On second thought, don't — every guy in town will be after her!"

"I think he's trying to tell you the bread and the stew smell good," Woody said. "He's too polite to ask for samples."

Mrs. Barrie laughed good-naturedly and asked Kim to get some plates out. She dished up stew for everyone. "Any cook worthy of the title always enjoys seeing people savor the product of her creativity," she said, helping herself to some ragout as well.

"What she means is, Woody ate most of it anyway, so she'll have to start over on dinner," Kim told Brenda and Brad. "But no fish fry, Mom. No fried anything for this party. Too much cholesterol — athletes try to stay away from it." She explained to the newcomers that they were trying to decide on a menu for a party they were catering at the Lawrences', "as in Chan Lawrence, the tennis star."

The group brainstormed for the few minutes it took to polish off both stew and bread.

The general consensus was that a barbecue with steak, roast corn, baked potatoes, homemade sourdough bread, an enormous tossed salad, and finally, apple pie and ice cream (by the ton) would be by far the best approach. Mrs. Barrie nodded her agreement.

"But before we go any further with this, I should really speak with the Lawrences," she said. "I'd like their approval on the menu, and I'd also like to take a look at their property; it might not be quite right for a barbecue set-up."

"Let's go right now!" Woody said enthusiastically. "I'd be more than honored to convey you two charming ladies in my old but trusty automobile — name your destination!"

"I think we'll be on our way," said Brenda, standing up and gathering an armful of plates to carry to the sink. "Although after this — " she patted her stomach and rolled her eyes " — the last thing I need is a submarine sandwich! Thanks, Mrs. Barrie, it was delicious!" She took Brad by both hands and pulled him to his feet.

Woody, Kim, and Mrs. Barrie quickly straightened out the kitchen, then headed outside for the red Volvo parked in the driveway.

Kim hopped in the back while Woody held the door to the passenger seat for Mrs. Barrie. "Where is this place, anyway?" he asked.

"Park Heights," she informed him.

Woody whistled as he started the car and pulled onto the street. Park Heights was the most exclusive section of Rose Hill; the homes there weren't houses, they were estates.

They reached the Lawrence place to find themselves confronted by a high, wrought-iron fence with gates. "Not the kind of friendly place where a person can drop in, sample the cooking, maybe even eat up the family dinner," Woody mused.

There was no street number, just a discreet bronze marker reading WILDCLIFF. "Wildcliff?" Kim said skeptically. "From what I can see, it looks like if each blade of grass has been cut individually!"

"The gate is closed," Mrs. Barrie observed. "Maybe we should have called for an appointment."

21

Woody grinned at his passengers. "Nonsense! You are about to have an appointment, unless I've lost my touch. Just leave it to me. Remember the Senator's wife?"

Kim laughed. She sure did remember! Woody had sweet-talked Mrs. Fitch while Kim, scared witless, had sneaked to the freezers in the basement of the Senator's to try to find a paper bag full of money. It was money she'd raised for the girls' track team at Kennedy High; it had gotten mixed in with bags of frozen food from Earthly Delights. What an escapade! That was the day Kim had really fallen for Woody, head over heels.

Woody slid out from behind the wheel, walked to the gate, and looked for a bell or buzzer. He found a phone and picked it up.

"Mrs. Barrie is here to see Mrs. Lawrence," he announced calmly. "Mrs. Barrie is the caterer. Yes, Earthly Delights."

He turned and winked at Kim and her mother. "No sir, I'm afraid this is the only free time she has." Now he gave them a thumbs-up sign. "Right. Thank you very much."

Woody bowed to the gates gravely as they opened by remote control.

"Mrs. Lawrence is home, Mrs. B., but apparently the Crown Prince is practicing with his coach. If we go out to the court, we're to tiptoe around so we don't disturb his concentration. Or else, it's off with our heads!"

The long driveway, paved with cobblestones and bordered with red and white flowers, curved sharply, and suddenly Kim caught her breath.

The house was before them — a three-story brick Georgian, with white pillars.

"It's mah-valous," observed Woody, pulling the Volvo into a covered side entrance. "Ladies," he said, grinning, "may I help you from your carriage?"

Kim half expected a butler to answer the front door, but instead they were greeted with a hearty smile by Mr. Lawrence, himself. He shook hands all around, then turned to look down the hall behind him.

A husky, deeply tanned young man with sun-streaked blond hair came toward them. He was shirtless and wearing tennis shorts, with a towel draped around his neck. His bronzed chest and face gleamed with sweat.

Kim had only seen pictures of Chan Lawrence, but she'd have recognized him almost anywhere. He was even more gorgeous than she'd imagined.

He glanced at the others, then looked right at Kim. He smiled and took her hand. "Well, hello there," he said, his ice-blue eyes piercing right through her.

Kim smiled back, her knees melting. Even after he'd released her hand, it still burned from his touch. She was in a daze during most of the tour of the kitchen and the grounds; the only time she came to life was when she caught another glimpse of Chan Lawrence, now back on the tennis court. But two things she was absolutely sure of: One, this was going to be *some* party. And two, when Chan Lawrence was near her, Woody Webster might just as well have been invisible.

Chapter
3

"Sasha, I have to talk to you," said Kim, bursting into the bookstore. Sasha looked up from the counter, where she'd been flipping through a publisher's catalog, surprised. She was used to Kim's high-energy entrances, but right now there was definitely something supercharged about her. She looked as if she'd been struck by lightning.

"What's the matter?" asked Sasha.

Kim hurriedly looked over her shoulder. "Woody's parking the car and I don't want to talk in front of him."

Sasha cut her short, puzzled. "Since when do you two have secrets from each other?"

Before Kim could continue, Rob Kendall entered the Albatross, proclaiming he had a serious case of writer's block.

Woody was right on his heels. He handed Rob a book on family medicine. "Try this," he suggested. "If you don't find a home remedy, maybe

Sasha will brew you some herb tea. That seems to cure just about everything."

Woody seemed nervous to Sasha, too. She was very sensitive to atmosphere, and this one was crackling. She wanted to get Woody and Kim talking about what was going on, but she didn't want to pry. She tried to be direct, but tactful. "You're steamy this afternoon, Mr. Webster. What's on your mind?"

"You know what's wrong with me, with all of us?" he answered, unconsciously hooking his thumbs in his suspenders in an orator's pose.

"It's that ol' summer vacation letdown. The crowd is fragmenting because we don't have school to keep us together. What we need is a group project. Whip up a little enthusiasm, work together at something."

He took a deep breath and went on. "All year long, we gripe about classes but we always have something else going on, like the Follies, football games, ski trips, the fashion show. Everybody's got their summer jobs now, and there's always the sub shop, but it isn't the same."

"You're right, Woody." Sasha nodded sympathetically. "I love working at the bookstore, but I miss that feeling of togetherness, too.

"Got any suggestions?" She knew she didn't even need to ask. Woody was an idea man; she could see the wheels already spinning.

"The Fourth of July is coming up," he answered promptly. "We could all go to D.C. to hear the Beach Boys and watch the fireworks. Kim could mastermind the ultimate Fourth of July picnic."

25

He turned to look at Kim, his arm reaching for her instinctively, but she wasn't participating in the discussion, instead seeming absorbed in a study of book titles a few aisles away. Sasha noticed her pick up a large book about tennis — she could see the cover photo — then drop it as if it had stung her.

"How about it?" persisted Woody. "Want to go to D.C. on the Fourth, Kim, my girl?"

"You said you went last year," she replied in a distracted tone. "You got caught in traffic for three hours on the way home! It sounds like it's more trouble than it's worth."

Sasha lifted her slender dark eyebrows at her friend. This was completely out of character; Kim was usually the most optimistic and adventurous of people. Sasha decided it was time to get to the bottom of things.

"Woody, would you watch the store for a couple of minutes?"

"Would Woody watch the store? Would he? Woody would," he answered. He made as if to vault over the counter.

Sasha giggled. "Come on, Kim. Back to the office. I want your opinion on something." She tossed a glance at Rob, who was restlessly pacing the stacks. She'd like to talk with him — maybe later, if he stuck around.

"Kiss me good-bye," Woody said in a stage whisper to Kim as she stepped around the counter.

"Not here," Kim whispered back, looking over at two women who were knee-deep in the latest shipment of paperback romances.

"They'd love it — vicarious thrills. And we

26

might shake what's-his-name with the glasses out of his writer's block." Woody put his arms around her.

Following Sasha, she pecked him quickly on the cheek, then slipped free, back to the privacy of the little office.

"Okay, what's going on, Kimberley Barrie?" asked Sasha, pointing to a straight-backed chair and sitting down herself behind her father's cluttered desk. "Did you and Woody have a fight?"

"Nobody could fight with Woody!" Kim groaned. "He's such a pussycat." She searched for words. "You and Wes fell in love at first sight," she began slowly. "You just looked at each other, and zap, that was it. Isn't that the way it happened?"

"So?" Sasha prompted.

"Well, I looked at somebody today. And he looked at me the same way. It was like putting my finger in an electrical outlet. Sasha, I think I've fallen in love!" Kim looked stricken.

"And now you don't love Woody anymore?" Sasha couldn't hide her disbelief.

"But I do," said Kim. "At least I think I do. But this other guy . . . I just don't understand it. In just a few seconds it was like my whole world flip-flopped!"

Sasha fumbled around in her mind for something constructive to say. "Kim, is it Woody, is he smothering you again? Maybe you're only feeling a little claustrophobic, maybe you and Woody have been seeing too much of each other."

"No, it has nothing to with him," Kim said. "Sasha, you knew, with Wes. You knew it was forever and you thought you'd die if it didn't work out. You wouldn't let anything stand in the way."

For a moment, Sasha was speechless. It was almost as if Kim wanted Sasha to advise her to break up with Woody! "You said you still love Woody," Sasha reminded her.

Kim looked like she might cry. "You think I should give up on Chan?"

Chan Lawrence, so that's who it was. "You're talking about Chan Lawrence?" Sasha exclaimed. "Oh, Kim, don't leap before you look." Sasha pushed her chair back and went around the desk to put a comforting arm around her friend. "You don't even know this guy. And I'm not so sure there's even any such thing as love at first sight after all."

Kim drew in a breath. "Are you talking about me, or are you talking about yourself?" she sniffled. "Don't you love Wes? I thought he was so right for you."

"I don't know," Sasha admitted slowly. "I mean, I do still love him, but now and then I feel as if we're not on the same wavelength anymore. Maybe we never were. Sometimes I can't help thinking we might be better off with other people."

Sasha was startled when a picture of Rob popped into her mind. She'd only met him this morning! And all she really knew about him was that he loved books and wanted to be a writer, like she did. There certainly hadn't been any sparks involved in that particular first encounter, just the relaxed, enjoyable sense that they had something in common, could become friends.

"What am I going to do?" asked Kim. She laughed a little at herself now.

Sasha knew there weren't any easy answers. "I think the best thing to do is to do nothing at all. Just go with things, see what happens. Don't do anything hasty that you might regret. You know Woody is too important to you to just let him go."

Kim smiled weakly.

"Give yourself some time — you'll figure out your feelings sooner or later," concluded Sasha. "And speaking of Woody, I forgot all about him!"

Sasha scooted back to the front counter. "Woody," she began.

He cut her off, finger to his lips. He'd turned on the radio and now he pointed to it.

"The Rose Hill Humane Society needs your help, all you animal lovers," said a voice. "It is absolutely essential that we come up with additional funding. We're overcrowded. It's quite literally a matter of life and death. We have to expand our facilities or we'll be forced to put puppies and kittens to sleep."

Sasha gasped and tears sprang to her eyes. "That's horrible! I thought they never put any animals to sleep."

"We need money. We need homes for some of our animals," the voice continued.

"Okay, there's our project," said Woody, snapping off the radio. "Agreed?"

Kim and Sasha both nodded enthusiastically.

"But how can we help specifically?" Kim wondered.

Woody didn't miss a beat. "We'll have a dog

wash — we'll do cats, too — horses — whatever! Bring your pet to the Humane Society and we'll wash and groom it for three or four bucks. Like the car wash we ran at school!"

Sasha was amazed at how the idea lifted her spirits. Kim was grinning, too. Both girls were always eager to be involved in a good cause.

"Publicity," Sasha said. "We want to draw everybody there, even people who don't have pets. Those are the ones who just might adopt."

"Posters. Radio spots!" Kim chimed in. "I'll call Monica — she can announce it on her spot on K100."

"That's a good idea!" Woody threw his arms around Kim, who couldn't help smiling.

Sasha was happy to see that Rob had approached, a book in his hand. He walked lightly, like an athlete. He wasn't that big, but he still looked more like a football player than a bookworm. Now he waved the paperback volume in her direction.

"I decided to take this Isaac Asimov after all," he said to Sasha. "And I couldn't help overhearing — I think a pet wash is a great way to help out the Humane Society. Best of luck with that!"

Sasha had rung up his purchase on the cash register and after she handed him his bag he turned to go.

"Good luck with your writing?" she called. He waved back at her. He seems like such a nice guy, Sasha thought, glancing idly at her watch.

"Five o'clock!" she gasped. "Closing time! Where has this day gone! Wes'll be here any minute to pick me up for dinner!"

Woody had a pencil in his hand. "Let's just get a few of the details down, okay?"

First they had to choose a day. "How about Saturday of Fourth of July weekend? Everybody free? Or does that conflict with the bash at the Lawrences', Kim?"

"No, that's this Friday," she said. "I'm free."

Sasha would simply ask her parents for the day off, knowing in advance that they'd approve of a good cause. Mr. and Mrs. Jenkins were veterans of causes. Ban the bomb, save the whales, feed the poor; they really cared about the state of their world and everyone in it. Some of Sasha's earliest memories were of marching in peace parades with her parents, carrying her own little banner and riding on her father's shoulders when she got tired.

"Okay, then, Saturday the second of July," said Woody. "First we have to rally the troops for a planning session. How about later tonight?"

He scribbled three lists, one for each of them with the names of friends to call. Chris and Ted, Brenda and Brad, Peter and Monica, Henry Braverman and Janie Barstow, Phoebe and maybe her friend Michael. And Wes, of course. He put Wes on Sasha's list with a heart drawn next to his name.

Sasha was happy at the prospect of Wes having a chance to be part of her crowd. Even though he got along well with her friends, the fact that he went to Leesburg meant that he missed out on a big part of their camaraderie. The pet wash was really shaping up to be a good time.

She glanced at Woody and Kim. Their heads

were close together and Kim was laughing as Woody drew a funny picture on her list. Woody had been exactly right, Sasha thought. They really did need this activity. What he didn't realize, though, was that his relationsip with Kim might depend on it.

After picking her up at the bookstore, Wes stopped with Sasha at her house so she could change for dinner. They were going to the American Cafe. Wes was dressed in white flannels and a navy blue cotton sweater. He looked terrific, Sasha thought. She didn't realize she'd matched her new shell pink blouse with white jeans, too, until Wes pointed it out to her.

"You see?" He grinned. "We really match, you and me." Sasha's parents were still out, and she and Wes were alone in the living room. He put his arms around her, then tilted her chin up. His lips came down on hers, gently at first, then hungrily.

Sasha abandoned herself to his embrace. As always, kissing Wes set her blood on fire. No matter what she might be thinking in her head about their relationship, his touch erased anything but the intense feeling that they did match — they fit together perfectly.

But on the way to the restaurant in Wes's father's flashy Corvette, some of the magic faded. Wes announced that everything was squared away with his parents — they understood why Sasha couldn't visit the cottage today.

"So we've switched plans," Wes went on. "Saturday is pet wash day and I'll be there to help. But after that, we'll head over to Sherwood Forest and spend the rest of the long weekend."

"Sherwood Forest?" Sasha repeated.

"You'll love it," he said. "It'll be a great weekend. My folks are planning to have a crowd. Some of the junior officers and their wives will be there. It'll be a terrific chance for you to talk to them, get an idea of Navy life, from the woman's point of view."

Sasha thought it sounded horrible, but she bit her tongue. She didn't want to speak too hastily, especially since Wes appeared to feel very strongly about the subject.

"I'll be out of place," she began.

"Not so," Wes assured her. "That's one of the things I want you to experience firsthand. The Navy is a family. You'll be gathered right in, you'll feel right at home."

They'd been over this ground before, and Sasha had thought she'd made it clear to Wes that while she loved him, loved being with him, she didn't want to have any part in the military side of his life. She respected his sense of honor, but she just didn't feel she could pretend to enjoy a welcome into a "Navy family" that had to be so foreign to her own beliefs about what was right.

She turned to Wes and studied his handsome profile. He was intent on driving. He drove carefully and seriously; in fact that was the way he did just about everything. Sasha put a hand on his shoulder and took a deep breath.

"Wes, I'd love to spend a weekend with your parents at the shore; it really does sound like a lot of fun. But I'm not sure I'm ready to be inducted into the Navy family. You know how I feel about that. And you and I always get along so much better when we keep our relationship apart from all of that — " Sasha searched for the right word, " — stuff."

Wes shot her a puzzled glance, but spoke firmly. "Sasha, I'd just like you to meet some of these people. They're my parents' friends, and mine, too. And my parents refuse to let another week pass without meeting you! It's my world, Sash — it's important to me that you fit in."

Sasha softened instantly. She couldn't be pushed, be forced to fit in, but if she cared about Wes she owed it to him to be open-minded.

"Okay?" asked Wes, pulling into the restaurant parking lot. He cut the engine, then put his arms around her, kissing her tenderly.

"Okay," she said.

Wes was happy and relaxed during dinner. The meal was perfect. And Wes was sweet and attentive: asking her how her food was, would she like some more water, complimenting her, touching her hand across the table, putting his sweater around her shoulders when she was cold, insisting that they share a big, chocolate-y, unhealthy dessert.

Sasha studied Wes through her eyelashes, and she couldn't help but see what had first attracted her to him so strongly. Those deep-set green eyes, the broad shoulders, the muscular build. Suddenly she remembered their very first dinner together and her eyes brightened with tears.

"I love you," she said, a tremor in her voice.

Wes reached over to take her hand. "I love you,

too, Sasha Jenkins, for always. You're my O.A.O. That's Navy slang for One and Only. Let's get out of here."

He called for the waiter and paid the bill, then propelled her out the door in a hurry. Once outside, he took her in his arms, held her close, and buried his face in her soft, dark hair.

"I really do love you." His voice was hoarse. "If the Navy wasn't in my blood so deep, I'd think seriously of going civilian so we could get married next year, go to college together."

Sasha was too stunned by Wes's mentioning marriage to wonder if there really was a chance that he'd ever give up the Navy. Later, when she thought about that moment, still tingling from Wes's touches and his words, she realized she would never want to be the one to talk Wes out of his dream of being a Navy pilot. She knew the value of dreams, even if his dream sometimes made him a stranger to her.

"Let's get back for the meeting," she said. She was a little afraid of the emotion Wes was feeling and that he was stirring in her.

"Kid stuff," he murmured.

Maybe exactly what we both need, she thought.

Chapter
4

The meeting was at Kim's house because, as Woody had pointed out, the best food in town was at the Barries'.

Walking to the front door from the driveway, Sasha clung to Wes's hand. He had practically asked her to marry him! It was scary and she wasn't close to being ready for a permanent commitment — but even the thought of it made her feel different.

She rang the bell and the door opened a crack.

"Sorry, we're not interested in whatever you're selling," said Woody, starting to close the door.

"Sorry." Wes laughed. "We were looking for the think tank, not the kindergarten. We'll go quietly." He turned away.

Woody's long arm reached out, snatched him by the collar, and dragged him inside. Sasha, still attached to Wes's hand, giggled as she found herself practically pulled off her feet.

36

The meeting was on the back porch, one of the most comfortable porches in town. It even had a big, creaky swing. Chris Austin and Ted Mason were perched on it, arms around each other like an old-fashioned courting couple.

"First, I want to make an announcement," Woody began. "We all burst out of school like that pious fellow from Liberia. Remember him?"

"Was he the oné in my algebra class?" Ted egged Woody on. Chris slapped him playfully. Woody dismissed him with a grandiose wave of the hand and cleared his throat to recite a limerick.

"There was a young monk in Liberia,
whose life went from dreary to drearier,
till he broke from his cell, with a hell
of a yell, and eloped with the Mother
Superior!"

The gang groaned loudly; somebody threw one of Mrs. Barrie's homemade oatmeal cookies at Woody.

Woody continued, unruffled. "The juniors of Kennedy High, and our honorary senior — " Woody bowed to Brad, " — and our honorary cadet, burst out of the prison of school a lot like that, but once liberated we sort of collapsed. Summer's supposed to be fun, right?"

He was answered by a chorus of "right" with someone throwing in a "left" for good measure.

"So we're going to get down to the business of having fun in our favorite way — the big, all-together way — with this pet wash to benefit the Rose Hill Humane Society. What do you say, Henry and Janie? With you in on the act, we're sure to go in style."

There were more groans and laughter.

"Sure, Woody. Wash that dog, scrub that cat," said Henry with a smile.

"It's all for a good cause, folks," Woody concluded. "We can make a difference in the lives of countless little puppies and kittens that have been abandoned and taken in by the shelter."

"Meow," said Brenda, softly. Sasha glanced at her, her eyes lit with understanding. Brenda knew what it felt like to be unwanted.

Brad gave Brenda's hand a supportive squeeze. For some reason, it gave Sasha a pang, almost of envy. At first glance, Brad and Brenda seemed to be opposites; he was so conservative while she was a rebel. But underneath they were alike; they were caring people with strong principles.

Sasha glanced at Wes. Not a hair on his neat dark head was out of place. Would Wes support her if *she* ran away from home, had doubts, rebelled? Somehow, she doubted it.

"Now, I'll turn over the mike to my right-hand woman, our very own Pheeberooni!"

Phoebe Hall laughed as she was greeted by a chorus of claps and whistles. She sat on the picnic bench next to Kim — Woody's two girls, Sasha couldn't help thinking. Phoebe had long been a special friend of Woody's; once he'd had a hopeless passion for her.

Phoebe pushed back her long, thick red hair and smiled. "I guess we just need some volunteers, now," she said. "Mr. Woodpecker — I mean, Mr. Webster!" — more applause — "has outlined the general plan of action. You've all got special talents — let's hear how you think you can use them." She helped herself to some popcorn from the bowl Kim was passing.

Brenda spoke up first. "I could make a poster. Maybe draw a picture of a dog or something. We could make copies and put them up all over town."

Everyone began talking at once — Peter and Monica volunteered to write a radio spot and Monica would submit it to K-100; Kim was going to organize a hot dog and refreshment stand; Brad and Chris, the outgoing and incoming student body presidents, would use their political savvy to get pet shop owners to donate flea shampoos and grooming equipment.

Sasha was already mentally outlining a feature story, which she planned to submit to the Rose Hill newspaper. Just then she felt a tug on her sleeve. It was Wes, and his eyes told her very clearly that he was ready to leave. The other kids were all talking and clowning; the meeting was pretty much over.

When Wes dropped her off at her house, his good-night kiss was lingering and insistent, but suddenly all Sasha could feel was tired. It had been a long day, but she couldn't quite put her finger on what it was that made it seem like something had changed since this morning, when she'd danced with joy on the sidewalk in front of the Albatross.

Bright and early the next morning, Sasha rode her bike over to the Humane Society, her camera in her backpack, to get material for her newspaper article.

She almost wished she hadn't. The first thing that met her eyes was a row of chain-link runways, enclosing dogs of every description.

The minute they saw her, they surged against the fencing, tails wagging madly and barking for all they were worth.

Sasha parked her bike and approached the pens to be met by dozens of pairs of desperately hopeful dog eyes. It was as if each animal was saying, "Talk to *me*. I love you. Please adopt *me*."

Sasha got down on her knees, to talk to an adorable disheveled puppy who threw kisses at her with his eager tongue. She pulled out her Nikon and snapped a picture of him, his paws up on the fence, gazing imploringly at her.

Sasha stepped back and took an all-encompassing shot as well. But as a journalist she knew that the first one, of the lone puppy, would most effectively accompany her essay. It was a fact that depictions of mass starvations didn't always touch readers, whereas the story of one hungry child could melt the coldest of hearts.

Sasha now tore her eyes away from the homeless dogs and scanned the rest of the Humane Society complex. The building *was* small, a plain, one-level structure. There was plenty of room for an addition, though.

She was eager to see inside the building, but as she turned to head for the main entrance, the Humane Society truck pulled up right next to her. A uniformed driver got out and walked around to the back to open the doors. Sasha followed and looked over his shoulder. There was a cage inside, with a terrified little puppy cowering in the corner. He was black and brown and so young he could have fit in Sasha's pocket. Her heart melted.

"Where did you find him?" she asked the driver, an older man.

"He was running loose right down the middle of the street," he said, reaching in to retrieve the pup.

Of their own volition, Sasha's hands reached out and took it from him. She cuddled the tiny dog to stop its shivering. "There, there, baby. We'll take care of you," she assured him. A little pink tongue touched her cheek; Sasha was hooked.

"I think I just got adopted," she told the driver with a rueful smile. But she seriously couldn't bear the thought that this might be one of the animals the Humane Society would have to put to sleep if they didn't raise enough money for an addition to their shelter soon.

The man reached out and gently rubbed the puppy's ears. "Not this one," he told Sasha. "At least not for five days. She's wearing a collar, with an ID. If the owners don't call us, we'll try to locate them."

Sasha was both glad and sorry. She accompanied the driver into the concrete block building, the lost puppy still cradled in her arms. They entered a small and cluttered, but cheery room, crammed with file cabinets, chairs, and a desk with a typewriter and telephone. A volunteer greeted Sasha with a smile that faded to sadness when she saw the dog in her arms.

"Please don't tell me you want to give up your

own puppy," she said. "Honestly, we just can't — "

"It's not mine." Sasha hurried to assure her. "The driver of the truck found her."

"Sorry to jump on you like that," the woman apologized with a laugh. "Things are just getting so frantic around here. My name is Helen, by the way. Let's see if we can get this little gal taken care of."

Sasha handed the puppy to Helen, who checked the tag and reached for the phone. Before she could dial, a woman and her small daughter entered the office. When the little girl saw the puppy, she snatched it happily from Helen's arms.

"She fell out of the window," she said, hugging her pet close. "She likes to ride with her head out."

Sasha felt like snatching the poor puppy right back. As for the lecture, Helen beat her to it.

"Never, *ever* let your pet lean out the window," she said, addressing both mother and child. "I know dogs seem to enjoy it, but the wind pressure is bad for their eyes. They can also get dirt and other foreign particles in their eyes. And as you just found out, they can fall out the windows and be killed, or at the very least, get lost."

"Bring him back on July second for a dog wash," Sasha called after them.

She was talking to their backs. The woman had given her a nod of thanks and the two were now heading out the door with their pet.

"I can't imagine being so abrupt with someone who saved the life of my pet." Sasha turned back to Helen, shaking her head.

"Fortunately, that type of person is the exception rather than the rule. Most people are so grateful when they find their pets here safe and sound, that they leave a few dollars as a donation to the Society."

"That reminds me!" Sasha exclaimed, her fair skin pinkening with embarrassment. "You must think I'm pretty forward, advertising my dog wash without asking you about it first." She laughed at Helen's puzzled expression. "Some friends and I would like to have a fund-raiser for the Humane Society: We thought of a 'pet wash,' where people could bring their dogs and cats for a bath and some grooming. We may be amateurs when it comes to the finer points, but we've got lots of elbow grease. And if we could set up here, on the little lawn out front, we might be able to draw some people in to look at the animals and maybe even adopt one!"

Sasha's face was glowing now from excitement at the thought of really getting to work at raising money for such a good cause. Helen nodded enthusiastically. "I'd have to get the supervisor's permission for you, but that won't be a problem at all!"

The buzzer at the front desk alerted Helen to another visitor; as she and Sasha headed back to the lobby, Sasha asked, "You wouldn't really put animals to sleep, would you?"

"I'd rather take them all home," Helen said, with a laugh. "But we already have as many pets as my children can take care of and play with. I'm afraid if we don't expand the shelter soon, we will have to put to sleep the animals that have remained unclaimed for the longest period of time."

Sasha had enough notes for her article now; she thanked Helen and headed outside to her bike. It was still a beautiful morning, but somehow she didn't feel as bright and airy as she had on her way over.

She pedaled now to the Albatross, dropping her roll of film off at the Camera Craft on the way. Her loose lavender shorts billowed around her legs as she sped through the streets of Rose Hill.

Mrs. Jenkins was holding the fort at the bookstore when Sasha got there. Coming through the door, Sasha saw her mother behind the counter, deep in conversation with a young man. His back was turned, but he was wearing what was apparently his summer uniform: cutoffs, today with a Hawaiian-print shirt. Sasha recognized Rob Kendall's long, muscular, tanned legs.

"Hi, Mom," she said, swinging her knapsack from her shoulder. "Hi, Rob."

Rob flashed Sasha a big grin. He wasn't spectacularly handsome, she noted, but he was nice-looking. And that smile. . . .

"I'm selling my soul for a stack of books," he said, gesturing to a number of paperbacks on the counter.

"You're not kidding!" Sasha laughed. "Did you ever think of reading just one at a time? That would save you some money." She tipped her head sideways to read the titles he'd selected. There was another Asimov, a volume of Thoreau, *A Walking Tour of Georgetown*, a book on the history of photography in America, and a reference guide to literary agencies and publishing companies in New York City.

"What's the common denominator?" Sasha asked Rob. "I'm not much at sleuthing — I can't figure out what you could possibly be writing about from this selection."

Rob laughed. "There's really no mystery — I like to read everything I can get my hands on. As for writing, I just confessed to your mother that I'm attempting a novel. It's hard work, I'll tell you that much."

Rob was leaning against the counter, looking from Sasha to Mrs. Jenkins and back again as he spoke. His manner was both polite and natural; Sasha thought her first impression had been right — it would be fun to get to know him better.

"Rob is from Connecticut, Sasha," Mrs. Jenkins added. "He was just telling me that his father went to college with Ned Bennington, Laurie's father, and Ned arranged for him to house-sit this summer for a neighbor of the Bennington's."

"It's working out great," Rob said enthusiastically. "I go to school in Maryland, but I've never really taken the opportunity to explore Washington. It's a fun change to be so near the city. And I have the whole summer ahead of me to put this novel together. Right now," he looked at his watch, "I should get back to Bonnie."

Sasha raised her eyebrows.

"That's my friend, the Petersons' dog." He gave her a wink.

"Speaking of dogs," Sasha said, "maybe you'd like to bring Bonnie to our pet wash to raise money for the Humane Society on Saturday."

"That's right. I remember hearing you talking about that with your friends yesterday." Rob was rifling his pockets for money to pay for his books. "Saturday's the second, isn't it? I might . . . have plans. A friend of mine is going to be in town for the weekend, but — sure, I'll try to make it! If nothing else, I'll leave a donation for you here at the bookstore."

"That would be nice of you," Sasha said. She fingered the barrette that held back her long, silky hair. She was curious about Rob, the way he lived and the things he did. He was in college, he was a *novelist* . . . ! It was probably a college buddy who'd be visiting that weekend, maybe even a girl friend.

"It was nice to meet you," Rob said to Mrs. Jenkins as he turned to leave, books in hand. "Talking to you both has charmed me out of my writer's block."

"The only way to write is to apply the seat of the pants to the chair, or so they say," Mrs. Jenkins chuckled.

"Which reminds me, Sasha, the typewriter is in the office, at your disposal. I understand you have an article to write."

"Yes, mother," she said sweetly.

"And you," Mrs. Jenkins said to Rob, "get back to that novel."

"Yes, mother," he answered, grinning.

"Kids these days!" Mrs. Jenkins threw her hands up in mock despair. In her jeans and T-shirt, Sasha thought affectionately, she could have passed for a college student herself.

Chapter
5

Sasha was at the breakfast table the next morning, slicing a peach into a bowl of yogurt, when Wes knocked on the back door. He smiled at her through the window and she waved at him to come inside. To her surprise, Chris and Ted were with him. Both boys were dressed casually but neatly in long pants, and Chris was wearing a slim, pale yellow cotton skirt with a matching boxy, broad-shouldered jacket, her bright blond hair smoothly perfect as always.

Sasha whistled. "Good morning! You really don't have to look so nice just to stop by for a cup of herbal tea. Come on in, you guys!"

Mrs. Jenkins called a greeting from the kitchen, where she was toasting a bagel.

"Guess what, Sash?" Wes opened. "I've got a job teaching sailing to a whole bunch of little Navy juniors at a marina near Sherwood Forest."

Sasha shot out from the table to give him a

congratulatory hug. "That's terrific! Is that why everyone's all dressed up?" she asked teasingly. "I knew it had to be a special occasion."

Wes looked at her blankly. "We're going over to Annapolis today, remember?"

Sasha clapped her hand to her forehead. She'd completely forgotten the plans she'd made with Wes when they spoke on the phone the previous afternoon.

"Chris and Ted are joining us," he explained. "Ted mentioned that he'd like to look around and this seemed like a perfect time to give him a tour. What's the matter, aren't you still free?"

"Of course I am," she said promptly. "I'm just also still half asleep." She looked down at the baggy sundress she'd thrown on that morning and then back at her neatly dressed friends.

"One of these things is not like the other, huh?" Chris giggled.

"I don't suppose I can go like this — can you guys wait a few minutes more while I run upstairs and change? Ted, help yourself to a bagel."

Ted looked up at her. He'd already smothered a cinnamon-raisin bagel in cream cheese and now he stopped in mid-chew to give her a guilty, chipmunk-cheeked smile.

Chris mussed his golden brown hair.

"He's a good sport," she said fondly. "Feed him and he'll follow you anywhere."

The two girls went upstairs to Sasha's bedroom. As Sasha rifled through her closet for her new Laura Ashley dress, she realized that she was relieved to have Chris and Ted coming along on this day trip. When Wesley had first mentioned

48

it, her reaction had been negative. She had no desire to see Annapolis.

But the more she thought about it the more she realized she was being closed-minded. She was disapproving of something she had never even seen with her own eyes. And it was silly to be afraid that somebody was going to lock the Academy gates once she was inside. It wasn't as if she was in any danger of joining up.

Sasha giggled at the thought of herself as a Navy recruit. Chris looked up from Sasha's photo album and smiled. She was lightly tapping one white-pumped foot on the floor.

"That's a beautiful dress, Sasha," she commented. "I love the print."

"And it's so cool and comfortable," Sasha agreed.

Yes, it was going to be nice to have Ted and Chris along, Sasha decided, slipping her feet into a pair of flat sandals, then running a comb through her long, wavy hair. Things being the way they were with Wes — so intense lately — she was glad to have some of the pressure off her.

They were driving in Wes's mother's car, a roomy Buick. The windows were wide open and the radio was blasting. Sasha was beginning to feel like this was going to be a fun day. The swirling cool summer air exhilarated her.

"It is sort of silly to live an hour away from the state capital and never even visit it," Chris was saying.

It was a gorgeous day. Traffic was light and by skirting D.C., they made the trip in an hour on Route 301. Wes worked the car through the narrow streets until they came to broad Maryland Avenue and one of the gates to the Academy. He slowed. A guard gave the car a quick glance, then snapped a smart salute.

"How come he saluted you?" asked Ted. "You're not in uniform."

"He's a VIP," Sasha laughed. "Anybody could tell that just by looking at him. Probably a CIA agent."

"Sorry to disappoint you," Wes said with a grin. "He was saluting the car. The Navy sticker on the windshield indicates that my dad's an officer."

They parked and almost before they'd spilled out of the car, Wes was off at a quick pace.

"Hey, wait," Chris called. "Look over there, at that domed building. Something's going on."

"That's the chapel," Wes said. "It looks like a wedding."

The two girls wanted to get a closer look. As they approached, Sasha realized that there were two rows of officers standing on the stairs, their swords forming an arch.

It was a lovely picture. The bridegroom was in dress whites, the bride in a lacy, flowing gown. The bright morning sun glinted on the crossed swords, and the breeze, fragranced by early summer blossoms, caught the confetti tossed by the wedding guests and whirled it high into the air like handfuls of stars.

Wes held Sasha's hand tight. She turned to him, her eyes misty with emotion. He was standing tall, his own eyes glowing with pride. He does belong here, Sasha thought suddenly. He fits in so beautifully. She looked back at the wedding party just as the bride tossed her bouquet amid squeals of laughter. *And that could be me.* . . .

Chris was also mesmerized by the tableau. Now the newlyweds were posing for pictures beneath the arch of swords. Chris had stars in her eyes.

"If you get married here, promise me I can be your maid of honor," Chris whispered to Sasha.

"I wouldn't mind going to school here," Ted said suddenly.

"You?" Chris turned to him in surprise. "You've never mentioned wanting to interview here."

Ted laughed. "I'm the quarterback at Kennedy High, remember? Roger Staubach was quarterback for Navy back in the sixties, one of the greatest quarterbacks of all times. I wouldn't mind following in his footsteps. And, don't forget, Roger the Dodger went on to the Dallas Cowboys."

"If you're really interested," Wes told him, "my dad could help you try for an appointment. Chris could even help you since she works for our congressman — they make some of the appointments, too. We should talk about it sometime."

Ted nodded, his eyes taking in the scenes of Annapolis: the stern, classic architecture, the beautifully landscaped grounds, the intriguing uniforms of the cadets, both men and women. It was clear to Sasha that he had caught a measure of Wes's enthusiasm; his imagination had been sparked. And from the look of things, Chris

51

might just be all for such an ambition on Ted's part. Sasha knew that Chris was sometimes frustrated by Ted's laidback style; going to college at Annapolis would certainly be an exercise in discipline and self-direction.

The four were now crossing a large lawn. Chris had taken off her jacket as the day warmed up; Sasha longed to take off her sandals and run around the grass in her bare feet. She smiled to herself. Not appropriate conduct, Midshipwoman Jenkins!

Wes pointed to an enormous gray building with wings going out in all directions. "That's Bancroft Hall, the largest dormitory in the whole world."

They tripped up wide steps to the main entrance; in the courtyard beyond was a statue of an Indian. Sasha, Ted, and Chris looked to Wes. "Tecumseh," he informed them. "The midshipmen throw pennies to him for luck before exams. Before the Army-Navy football games, too, for luck. You know about that rivalry, don't you, Ted? It's the big one."

"Sure," said Ted.

"Even I know that," Sasha teased.

"And those bells, Ted?" Wes pointed enthusiastically at the enormous bells that flanked the steps of the Hall. "This is right up your alley — victory bells.

"You give us a win against Army and those bells will ring for days!"

Ted's eyes lit up. Wes pressed his point, with a wink at Chris.

"Every single member of the team even gets to ring the bell once. Sort of grabs you, doesn't it? It sure would be fantastic if you were on the team."

A group of young men and a few women in uniform marched by them in formation. Their crisp navy blue jackets practically shone, they were so perfectly pressed. Sasha couldn't imagine ever looking quite so neat.

Chris didn't understand. "Who are all these people?"

"Plebes," Wes said. "That's what they call freshmen."

"But it's summer. Why are they in school?"

"Plebes are sworn in in June and go through preliminary training all summer," Wes explained.

"Does that mean what I think it means?" Sasha asked him, a funny feeling in her stomach.

He nodded. "It means I'll be right here next summer. Weekdays, weekends, holidays." He took her hand gently. "It will be hard for us, not seeing much of each other, but it's worth it, Sasha."

Ted and Chris were holding a whispered conversation. They both burst out laughing.

"I just decided that if Ted tries for an appointment here, I'll try, too," Chris announced. "I'm not going to hang out, twiddling my thumbs in Rose Hill waiting to see him. I'm going to be right here with him instead! How does that sound?"

She began to giggle helplessly, clutching Ted's arm.

That struck Sasha as funny, too. "You're not serious about signing up though, are you, Chris?"

"Oh, I don't think so," she said when she'd

caught her breath. "I want to go into law or politics — I want a good education but I also want the freedom to spend time in activities outside of school. But this sure is an impressive place. It kind of sweeps you off your feet, you know what I mean?"

Yes, Sasha thought, I do. It's a lot like Wes that way.

By now they were all a little footsore and very hungry. Ted was complaining that the rumblings in his stomach sounded a lot like the roar of the crowd as Navy went ahead of Army by a touchdown in the fourth quarter.

"I know just the place for lunch," Wes assured him. He took them to a marvelous restaurant just outside the gates of the Academy, right down at the water's edge, where the four enjoyed a leisurely meal at an outside table. Sasha sighed contentedly as she sipped a tall glass of iced tea. It felt good to be outside of the Academy again; she just couldn't help but feel oppressed by the thought of living such a structured life no matter how glamorous it appeared.

After lunch Wes wanted to show them a few more things at the Academy, and after promising Sasha that they could then move on to a tour of St. John's College in another part of Annapolis, they headed back to the yard.

St. John's was a school that Sasha's parents had told her about; it was a seat of classical education, but it was also a progressive school — they didn't give grades, she told Wes, Ted, and Chris. Wes snorted. Sasha punched him playfully on the shoulder.

"I think it sounds fantastic," she said, seriously. "It sounds like a place where students can really explore their options and learn to express themselves."

Wes still looked doubtful.

"You know, Wes," said Sasha. Her voice was still gentle, but now there was an edge to it. "The structure and limitations of the military aren't for everyone."

Chris, Ted, and Wes all opened their mouths at once — Wes to defend the Academy, Chris and Ted to talk about anything but that. Just then they almost bumped into a familiar figure.

It was Rob Kendall. He greeted the group with a big smile and cheerful hello.

"What in the world are you doing here?" Sasha wondered with her head cocked to one side. "Somehow, I just don't believe you're a midshipman!"

He laughed. "No way. I do go to college in Annapolis, but this isn't the place."

"Don't tell me," Chris said, with a sly look at Ted. "St. John's?"

Wes smiled along with the others, but Sasha thought there was just a touch of scorn in his expression.

"That's right," said Rob. "I'm here now to use the Academy library — some research for my writing. They have an excellent facility here."

Ted waved his arms at the clear blue sky. "On a day like this you're going to the library?" He laughed. "I don't know about college, folks. It looks like once you go in, they don't let you out again!"

Rob shrugged with a good-natured grin. A piece of his longish hair had fallen forward over his glasses and he pushed it back with a gesture that struck Sasha as incredibly appealing. She glanced covertly at Chris; it was clear the other girl was also impressed with Rob's looks. Suddenly Sasha noticed Rob's feet — they were bare. His sneakers, the laces tied together, were slung over his shoulder along with his backpack. She giggled. Now that was a man after her own heart.

"It's not so bad," Rob was telling Ted. "I don't have a full-time job this summer so that gives me time to really get into my writing. So if I'm serious for a few hours during the day I can reward myself and play later on. Speaking of which, haven't I seen you before, playing ball for one of the local summer leagues?"

"Yeah, I'm with the Ramblers," Ted began, then looked at his watch with a start. "Folks, I hate to do this to you, but your day in Annapolis is officially over. It's three o'clock, and I have to get back for practice at four-thirty."

Chris saw that Sasha was disappointed that they wouldn't make it to St. John's. "We'll come back another time, Sasha. Maybe just you and me — I'd love to check out St. John's."

"You know," said Rob, his intense hazel eyes moving from Chris to Sasha, "I'd love to give you both a tour. It's a great place, but you need an insider along to make sure you get to all the right spots." He held Sasha's eyes and smiled. "St. John's could use a few girls as pretty as you two."

Ted laughed and threw his arms around Chris.

"It's the future freshman sensation of St. John's College," he teased. She blushed and rolled her eyes.

Wes had taken Sasha's hand possessively. "What do you say, gang, are we ready to go?"

"Yes, sir!" Chris saluted him.

"I'll be seeing you," Rob said, waving as he strode off toward the library. He'd probably been bored talking to high school kids, Sasha thought. He was as friendly as he could be, but no doubt he was happy to get on to all the important things he had to do.

She was surprised, then, to hear herself call him. "Rob, a bunch of us are meeting tonight at my house, to talk about the pet wash. Remember that?"

He stopped and stood looking at her. "Sure I do."

"If you want to come by — just for fun. . . . I live at Twenty-two Chestnut Street."

"That'd be great. Thanks Sasha. I've even had some experience with fund-raising at school — maybe I can give you a few tips." He waved and turned away.

Sasha felt frozen. She came back to reality with a start.

"Come on," Ted was saying, "last one back to the car is a rotten banana!" He grabbed Chris's hand and ran.

Wes and Sasha followed. Sasha shrieked when her sandal came off in the soft turf, but Wes was there to catch her in his arms. Suddenly the mood was light again.

They sang all the way home.

Chapter
6

"Earthly Delights," said Kim, picking up the kitchen phone. The Barries had a separate line there, especially for catering calls.

"Mrs. Barrie?"

"No, this is her daughter, Kim. May I help you?" Kim hitched up one of the straps on her rainbow-striped overalls.

"This is Mrs. Lawrence. I believe I met you the other day when you and your mother and a young man wearing red suspenders stopped by my house to discuss the party we're giving for my son, Chandler."

Kim smiled at the reference to Woody's eccentric attire. "Yes, Mrs. Lawrence, I was there. Do you have a question about the menu we decided on?"

"It's not just one thing, I'm afraid. It's everything. On thinking it over, Chan feels that a barbecue is wrong, quite wrong. He wants something more formal, and my husband agrees with him."

"Hmm." That was all Kim could come out with. She knew her mother was at the butcher's right now, picking up thirty pounds of strip steaks.

"Black tie," Mrs. Lawrence continued into Kim's silence.

Kim almost dropped the phone — a complete change of menu. Wait until her mother heard this! Some people.

She opened the drawer in the kitchen cabinet where the contracts with Earthly Delights clients were kept and pulled out the paper signed by Mr. Lawrence.

It was a temptation to read it to Mrs. Lawrence over the phone; at this point it was really a question of put up or pay up. Kim and her mom had already put in a lot of time on this party. But on second thought, Earthly Delights couldn't afford to lose such a big customer. Kim swallowed her steam.

"We'll be happy to make any changes, Mrs. Lawrence," she said as sweetly as she could.

"Aren't you nice. I was really worried about phoning you with such troublesome news. My husband and son were sure it couldn't possibly be a problem, but I find it difficult to make such demands of people."

Kim's face softened. Mrs. Lawrence sounded genuinely apologetic and it was obvious that none of this was her idea. When they'd toured the Lawrences' house the other day, Kim had observed — as much as she saw anything besides Chan Lawrence's brilliant white smile — that

Mrs. Lawrence stayed pretty well in her husband's shadow. And they were both eclipsed by their celebrity son.

"Why don't you drop over so we can discuss it?" Mrs. Lawrence continued, her voice warm. "I'd really appreciate your help in deciding upon a new menu for a formal sit-down dinner."

"It's really just a small list of changes," Mrs. Lawrence said. "I'd like to go over them today, and I must go out later. I was hoping you'd be able to come right over."

Well, why not? Kim thought. She was perfectly capable, and this way she could save her mother from a big headache.

Kim wasn't sure *she* was ready for another dose of Chan Lawrence, though. She'd recovered from the initial tailspin her crush had sent her into, and even regretted a little that she'd spilled her feelings so haphazardly to Sasha. She was curious to see how Chan would affect her the second time around.

Her mother had taken the car, so she'd have to bike it, as inappropriate as it might seem to arrive at the Lawrences' front gate on a ten-speed.

She left a note on the refrigerator to tell her mother where she'd be and turned on the telephone answering machine so Earthly Delights wouldn't lose any business in her absence.

Halfway out the door, she chickened out. She ran back to the phone and called the butcher shop just in case her mother might be there. No dice. Mrs. Barrie had already left. There was no telling where she might be now.

Kim knew Sasha had to work at the Albatross

today, but Phoebe worked at Arena Stage with Woody and had more flexible hours. She might just be home; Kim dialed her number quickly.

She gave a sigh of relief when Phoebe's bright voice answered the phone.

"Will you go with me to the Lawrences'?" she asked. "For moral support?"

"Sure," Phoebe said cheerfully. "I'd love to get a close-up look at our local celebrity. See how the other half lives."

Phoebe didn't have the use of a car, though. Her parents had the Audi at work.

"Well, it's far too much trouble for you to ride your bike, too," Kim decided.

"It might even be a breach of upper-class etiquette," Phoebe suggested. "I mean, one bike in the driveway is probably okay, but two — the butler would swoon in disapproval."

Kim laughed.

"I'll go if you really want me to," Phoebe added. "I could even wait outside the gates."

"No, you're right," Kim admitted. "There's no point in drawing attention to the fact that I'm a kid. I'm supposed to be a businesswoman! Thanks, Pheeb — catch you later."

Kim set off, assuring herself that biking was the way anyone who was anyone was traveling these days. At least it kept her in good shape. A tennis star's family had to appreciate that.

This time, the big iron gates were open. Kim swept in giving a good imitation of someone who felt she had every right to be there. She parked her bike by the side entrance. The door opened before she could reach for the bell.

Mrs. Lawrence had been waiting just inside. Now she held out her hand cordially. "Come in, dear. It's so nice of you to come."

She wasn't at all like her husband, Kim thought. He was a big man, florid and hearty. Chan was tall, too, and husky. Mrs. Lawrence was small and rather delicate, with fair hair and pale, powdered skin.

"Come into the sun room, dear," she said, tucking Kim's hand under her arm.

They were in an enormous central hall, with a magnificent curved stairway leading up to the second floor. Kim caught a glimpse of a formal dining room to the right. They turned left at a fork in the passageway.

"That's my husband's study," Mrs. Lawrence murmured, nodding to a closed door, as they passed through a huge living room with a marble fireplace and a many-tiered chandelier.

The sun room was beyond and seemed to be Mrs. Lawrence's domain. It was a homey room. The floor was flagged, the furniture was a bright, white wicker, and there were plants in profusion: a colossal split-leaf philodendron, a dracaena that touched the ceiling, a lacy palm, and several pots of blooming geraniums.

"It's lovely," Kim said, meaning it with all her heart.

Mrs. Lawrence was pleased. "Thank you," she said, smiling. "It's nice for me to have some company here."

She reached out and plucked off one faded red blossom and tucked it into the pocket of her immaculate polished-cotton Burma dress. Then she sat down on the couch and patted the cushion beside her.

"Business first," she said. "Before we get on to the menu for the formal dinner, dear, I must tell you that Chan and his father have changed their minds again. We'd like to have *two* parties — the barbecue as originally planned, so Chan can celebrate his nineteenth birthday with his friends, and a formal dinner at a later date.

"I'll sign a second contract right now, if you like, and then we can have a nice chat."

Kim was dazzled — things were really happening for Earthly Delights! She pulled a form from her knapsack and laid it on the glass-topped coffee table, then uncapped her pen and began to write in the information: customer's name and address, type of service required.

"Number of guests?" she asked.

"Oh dear, I'll have to check with my husband." Mrs. Lawrence fluttered her hands nervously.

"What about the date?" prompted Kim, smiling encouragement.

"Let's see . . . could you put down the last Saturday in the month? I'm afraid I can only be tentative. It all depends on whether my son will be playing an out-of-town match. My husband always travels with him, you know."

Kim reached a quick decision and put the cap back on her pen. "Mrs. Lawrence, I think it would be better if I just leave the contract with you so you and your husband can fill in the details. Then you can give us a call and either my mother or I will come back to discuss the fee for the second party and confirm both the menus."

"You're right dear, you're very right!" Mrs. Lawrence nodded vaguely. "Sometimes it's so difficult for me to keep things straight — with the family so often heading in two different directions. Chan's tennis takes up so much of my husband's time, and I have the home to take care of. . . ." her voice trailed off.

Kim smiled sympathetically and stood up to leave, but Mrs. Lawrence took her by the arm.

"Don't go yet." She looked hopefully at Kim. "Let's go out to the terrace. You can get a better idea of how to set up the barbecue when the time comes."

Kim was happy to comply; she followed Mrs. Lawrence outside. The brick-paved terrace fronted on a circular garden with a fountain. Beyond that were two tennis courts. When Mrs. Lawrence noticed Kim gazing eagerly in that direction, she led her across the garden, close enough to watch Chan as he worked out with his coach.

Chan was serving: back on his heels, forward on his toes; a perfect toss. Every muscle in his body stood out in magnificent relief; his racket seemed like an extension of his powerful right shoulder, arm and wrist, as it swung to meet the ball with a resounding thwack.

It was an ace. Kim caught her breath. She hadn't even seen it — the ball had moved so fast.

Chan moved across the court to serve to the other side. Now he was more or less facing Kim's direction. She could see the sweat dripping from his bright blond hair. Just as he tossed the ball, he caught sight of Kim; their eyes met and she could feel his concentration break. The serve was a dud.

The ball careened off his racket, right at her. Kim fielded it neatly and pitched it back to him.

"Nice catch," called Chan. "Nice throw."

He broke off practice, just like that, without even a glance at his coach, and strode to where Kim was standing with his mother. His feet seemed to act like springs; he was bursting with energy and athletic grace.

"I'm hoping Kim will stay for lunch with us, Chan," said Mrs. Lawrence, with a quick glance at Kim for confirmation. "Wouldn't that be nice?"

"I'm supposed to meet Cassie and company at the club," Chan said, his eyes crinkling at the corners. "I thought you knew."

"You'll just have to phone and excuse yourself, won't you, dear?" Mrs. Lawrence smiled shyly.

Chan laughed out loud and put an arm around his mother. He hadn't taken his eyes off of Kim. "She's so fragile-looking, isn't she?" he said to her. "Don't you believe it. My mother has a sneaky side."

Kim scuffed the toe of her running shoe. Chan was larger than life and while she felt charged by the magnetism he exuded, he also made her somehow feel small, more Mrs. Lawrence's size than her own five-foot-seven. She opened her mouth to excuse herself from lunch — she was just the caterer after all! — but nothing came out. With a flash of his bright white smile and a probing look from those blue eyes, Chan had struck her mute.

"Sometimes she comes up with an idea that's a real winner," he continued. "I'll go grab a shower. Promise you won't vanish the minute my back is turned, Kim."

He gave her a look that would melt any girl, and Kim was no exception.

"I'd love to stay for lunch, Mrs. Lawrence."

The minute Chan was out of sight, Mrs. Lawrence turned to Kim. "I hope you don't feel that I railroaded you into accepting my invitation, dear. 'Cassie and company!' Do you know who they are? They are four older girls, 'tennis groupies' I believe the term is. They follow him doggedly."

"Chan must find that very flattering," Kim said tactfully. "I guess that sort of thing happens to all celebrities, doesn't it?"

"It's outrageous," Mrs. Lawrence was shaking her head. "They have no manners at all. They make public spectacles of themselves. Complete lack of good breeding. I'd like for him to get to know some nice girls his age," she said with a wink.

Kim smiled at the compliment, but she was a little bit puzzled. Chan struck her as old enough to choose his own companions. Not that he'd exactly complained about his mother's substitution! It appeared to Kim that Mrs. Lawrence, who might seem to lack confidence in other directions, was ready to take the initiative when it came to Chan making the "right" connections. Cassie and company obviously didn't make the grade.

But why me? Kim wondered. Mrs. Lawrence seemed to like her, sure, but no stretch of anybody's imagination could turn Kim Barrie into high society. Maybe Mrs. Lawrence had just seized the chance to cut out the undesirable Cassie and company. Kim was amused at the thought of being used as a diversion. But for lunch with Chan Lawrence, I'd eat anywhere, under any circumstances, she thought.

Lunch was on the terrace, and although it was a light, simple meal, the elegance of preparation and presentation more than impressed the caterer in Kim. Earthly Delights couldn't put together anything better, she had to admit herself, as she sampled the cold cucumber soup, a fresh seafood salad with a fabulous dill dressing, and finally strawberries the size of her fist smothered in the lightest whipped cream imaginable.

For the most part, though, Kim wasn't even tasting the food that she lifted mechanically to her mouth. Mrs. Lawrence had somehow disappeared from the scene before the meal was served, and she was alone with Chan. When he'd first reappeared, his thick blond hair neatly combed but still damp, wearing pale yellow tennis shorts and a white polo shirt with a Nike patch on the sleeve, she had almost fallen off her chair. It didn't seem possible, but she could swear he got more gorgeous every time she saw him.

Now they were eating lunch, Chan sitting on the same side of the table as Kim, his chair so close to her that more often than not his knee was touching hers. She was so overwhelmingly aware of his physical presence that it was all she could do to chew and swallow properly. She wouldn't have been surprised if the forkfuls of crab and shrimp were missing her mouth entirely and dropping on her lap.

"So Kim, tell me about yourself," said Chan, putting his fork down, as if Kim's life story was sure to be the most fascinating thing he'd ever heard.

Kim briefly sketched an outline of her activities since she'd moved to Rose Hill, her plans for the summer, the take-off success of her mother's business.

"I really like Rose Hill," she concluded, her green eyes bright with enthusiasm. "I've made so many great friends here."

"Like that guy with the suspenders?" Chan raised one disdainful bleached-blond eyebrow.

"Oh, he's very nice — he just has kind of an unusual taste in clothes." Kim felt a little guilty of this minimal defense of Woody.

"I could introduce you to a lot of fun people," Chan said, not interested in pursuing the topic of Kim's friends, suspendered or otherwise. He placed a hand on her shoulder and squeezed it lightly. "Some really cool people."

Kim smiled weakly. Her shoulder and her heart were equally on fire. Chan made it sound like he wouldn't mind hanging out with her. Lunch at his house was one thing, being introduced to his gang, whoever that might be (Cassie and company?), would be something altogether different. She was eager to appear a worthy companion for Chan; her mind raced, and then she hit upon the obvious.

"I like sports," she began lamely. Oh, that's just brilliant, Kim, she chided herself. So what?

But Chan picked right up on it. "Do you play tennis?" he asked.

"Yes, but not exactly in your league," Kim laughed.

"Come on," he said, tossing his napkin on the table. "Let's knock a few balls back and forth, see how good you are."

Kim looked down at herself. Not only was she not wearing shorts, she was wearing rainbow-striped overalls. Just to make sure I look like a clown on the court, she thought ruefully. "At least I've got sneakers on," she said with a smile.

"Yeah, running shoes are no good for tennis," Chan was saying as they strolled to the courts. "They're dangerous. The flared heels restrict lateral movement — not a problem when you're running — and that puts stress on your knees and ankles."

"The volleyball coach at Kennedy High says the same thing," Kim agreed.

Kim unzipped the cover of the racket Chan had asked the maid to bring for her. It was beautiful; clearly the latest model. She had a decent graphite racket herself, but compared to this it might as well have been made of wood and strung with spaghetti. She couldn't imagine what it must have cost.

They faced each other across the net. Kim stood well behind the service line. She was sure Chan could make a monkey out of her with the first ball. And she was curious to see how he would play to her; if he was the kind of man who enjoyed ridiculing others, then he wasn't the man for her.

The first ball was an easy shot to her forehand. She returned it smoothly.

Chan could have smashed it back out of her reach or right at her feet, but he didn't. He sent her another easy forehand and they began to work up a rhythm. Now he tried her backhand; she made a one-handed return.

Chan started to put more power into his strokes. To Kim's delight, she still managed to keep the rally going, even though she felt slightly restricted by her overalls.

"Try a couple of serves," he suggested, hitting several balls over to her.

She picked up two and moved behind the baseline with her weight on her right foot, dropped both arms together, then tossed the ball up with her left hand winding up with her right.

The result was anything but spectacular. She hit the net on the first serve; the second one went over, but it was way out. Kim was embarrassed.

"Try again," suggested Chan with a smile. "Bend the elbow of your racket arm so the racket points straight up. Okay, now throw. Follow through with the swing and snap your wrist as you connect with the ball."

This one was much better; Kim was pleased and she glowed under Chan's compliments and admiring eyes.

"Not bad for a beginner!" he called to her from across the court with a teasing grin.

The next rally was interrupted by the reappearance of Chan's coach. Kim had learned over lunch that his name was Ned Thompson; he'd once made it to the quarter finals of the U.S. Open.

Now he called Chan aside with a curt nod in Kim's direction. Kim couldn't hear the conversation, but she could tell by their expressions that they were exchanging heated words.

Kim turned her back, pretending to be absorbed in bouncing a ball with her racket. She looked at her watch. She'd been at the Lawrences' for hours.

Chan rejoined her, his eyes still flashing with defiance. "I'll walk you to your car," he said firmly. "I have to get back to practice."

"Don't you get any time off?" Kim asked, as they skirted the house to get to the carport, where she'd left her bike.

"Not much," he admitted. "Today was special." He looked down at her. "You're special. I want to see you again, soon."

Kim's knees and ankles dissolved, and she tossed back her short, swingy brown hair to hide her confusion. She couldn't believe that Chan Lawrence was saying this to her!

"Well, there's the party on Friday. . . . My mom and I will be here to cater it — "

"That's much too far off," he insisted. "How about tonight?"

Kim's heart leaped and then fell like a stone. Tonight she had a meeting about the dog wash with the gang; and tonight and every night she had a boyfriend: Woody Webster, who would not be happy if she went out with another guy.

She felt herself blush. "Thank you, Chan, but I have plans tonight. Me and some of my friends from school are planning a fund-raiser for the

Rose Hill Humane Society." She giggled nervously. "A pet wash, actually. Sounds silly, huh? But anyway, we're meeting tonight to see how we're coming along with our plans."

"You're putting me on!" he scoffed. "A pet wash? You guys must be hard up for fun!" But before Kim could respond, Chan's attitude had changed. He softened his voice. "I mean, that does sound like fun. You know — " Kim was standing with her back to the wall of the carport, and now Chan placed a hand on the wall above her left shoulder and leaned close to her, " — that must be great being part of such a close group of friends. I've always been so busy with my tennis, sometimes I feel like I'm missing out socially. I have friends, but they're not *real* friends. I was never a normal teenager."

He was so near to Kim now that she could feel the warmth radiating from his skin. His confession had really moved her; here she was thinking that he was a super-cool celebrity, when he was really just like anybody else, even lonely.

"So can I bring my Doberman to your pet wash?" he asked with a provocative smile.

"Of course," Kim said sincerely.

"You know," Chan was clearly struck with a new thought, "I have an interview tomorrow with a D.C. TV station. I could mention your fund-raiser, maybe even say I was getting involved with it myself. That'd be fantastic publicity for . . . your pet wash."

"You could really do that?" Kim said excitedly. "You'd really like to take part in this?"

"Sure, I could sort of be your sponsor. It sure wouldn't hurt your cause."

"No, it would be great for publicity, Chan, you're right!"

"And it would give me a chance to spend some time with you, Kim, and I'd really like that. Somehow I think a girl like you would be really good for me."

Kim blushed again. She wouldn't have minded standing in the carport all day having Chan say things like that to her, but she knew her mom would be home by now and maybe even worried. Besides, she had other clients to call and parties to prepare for.

She slid the kickstand of her bike back and wheeled the ten-speed into the driveway.

"Are you sure you have time for something like this, Chan? I mean with your busy tennis schedule and all?"

Chan gave her a strangely confident smile. "I'll check it out with my coach. Somehow I have a feeling he won't mind."

Kim pushed off, very aware that Chan's eyes were following her as she pedaled away. She could imagine the look on Woody's face, on everyone's face, when Chan arrived at the pet wash! Kim gulped and pedaled faster.

She'd introduce the idea of Chan helping them out at tonight's get-together, see how it went over with the gang. Even Woody would have to see the merit in having a celebrity like Chan Lawrence serve as a sponsor, she told herself, lying through her teeth.

Chapter 7

Rob showed up at the Jenkins house that evening for the meeting. He checked his watch; he was a few minutes late. He felt a little funny about getting together with Sasha and her friends — not that a couple of years' age difference bothered him; he just hoped having an older guy around wouldn't cramp their style.

Mrs. Jenkins answered the door. "Oh, hi, Rob," she said, surprised. "Didn't anybody tell you? The whole crowd went down to the river in their bathing suits. They took enough hot dogs to feed an army."

He grinned. "So the dog wash planning session is off then?"

She chuckled. "I don't think so. I think they just decided that they could get any business done just as easily while swimming and picnicking."

Mrs. Jenkins pointed him in the right direction, and Rob headed for the river. The park, where people went to fish and swim, was about half a mile from the Jenkins' house.

He parked his black Renault Alliance alongside the other cars — ranging from Woody's faithful Volvo to Ted's red MG. He then scrambled down a steep path to the riverbank, where he could see a few kids swimming and splashing.

He found Sasha, Chris, Ted, and Wes wrapped up in damp towels, huddling close to the fire that would eventually burn down enough for grilling. Sasha gave him a welcoming smile. Rob couldn't help but notice that her boyfriend, Wes, looked far less cordial.

"If you're serious about getting appointed to the Academy," Wes was saying to Ted, "you really have to get cracking. The first of June is when most of the guys — and girls, of course — send in their application letters. I took care of that a while ago. You're already running late."

Ted nodded, munching on a handful of potato chips.

Sasha traced a circle in the sand. Rob could see that she was bothered by Wes's steamroller approach. "Aren't you pushing him a little, Wes?" she asked carefully. "I mean, just because he got carried away on a tour of the Academy doesn't mean — "

"Sure, I understand that," he interrupted her, "but time marches on. No kidding, you've got to write to your senator or your congressman, take competitive exams, fitness tests. . . . It'd be pretty easy to miss the boat, so to speak."

Chris and Ted howled at Wes's pun, and Rob smiled, trying to catch Sasha's eye, but she was still looking down, preoccupied. He watched her take a thick strand of her hair and squeeze the water from it; when Wes put a hand on her arm she didn't respond. Sitting there all wet and shivering and quiet, she suddenly struck Rob as very vulnerable, and very pretty.

"What about the dog wash?" Sasha asked, obviously hoping to change the subject. "Where's Woody and the rest of the gang?"

Chris pointed down to the river. Woody, Brad, Brenda, and Kim were having a splashing contest, while Monica and Peter watched from their perch on a fallen tree that stuck out over the water. Phoebe and Michael Rifkin, her voice teacher's son and a good friend, were walking further down on the shore, bending down occasionally to pick up pebbles for skimming.

"Yeah," said Ted, "we're never going to be ready by Saturday at the rate we're going."

"*This* Saturday?" Sasha nodded and Rob whistled. "I thought you were aiming for the next weekend," he said.

"It really doesn't give us much time, does it?" Chris agreed.

"You know, I think you should put it off for one week," Rob suggested, reaching for some potato chips. He glanced around the group. Only Wes wasn't listening attentively. "With some extra time for organization, you could turn this pet wash into a kick-off point for a major drive to raise money for the Humane Society, not just an end in itself."

"You're exactly right," Sasha said. Her eyes lit up, obviously inspired by the idea of directing their project toward a greater effort. Rob saw Wes glance at Sasha. For some reason her enthusiasm seemed to bother him.

He turned to Rob. "Who asked you, anyway?" he said. His tone was light, but something in his eyes told Rob distinctly that Wes didn't think he belonged there.

There was an uncomfortable silence.

Wes realized he'd gone too far and his usual politeness asserted itself. "Sorry," he said. "I didn't mean that the way it came out."

Rob shrugged good-naturedly. He was happy to let it pass, but Sasha spoke up, glancing at Chris for support.

"I invited Rob to join us, Wes," she said firmly, "because he's had a lot more experience with this sort of thing that we have. I for one really appreciate him sharing his opinions."

"I've already apologized," Wes said to her, his voice low.

"Okay! Let's go!" shouted Chris. "Everybody in for a swim!" She flung off her towel and ran for the water. She went in with a flat racing dive.

Sasha raced after her, while the three boys remained talking on the shore. Ted was telling a joke that made both Wes and Rob burst into laughter.

The two girls swam a few strokes, then slowed, treading water.

"What's eating Wes?" asked Chris, leaning back to float. "I never saw him like this before. The only time I ever heard him say a sharp word to anybody, much less to you, was at Ted's party that time when he got in a fight with John Marquette over the Leesburg-Kennedy football rivalry!"

"I don't know," Sasha admitted, shaking the water out of her eyes. "I really think it's this whole Annapolis thing — it has him so pumped up. Don't let him brainwash you and Ted with all his talk about the Stars and Stripes!"

Chris laughed. "You don't have to worry about me, I was only kidding about applying. And Ted may not always seem like he knows what direction he wants to head in, but he really has a mind of his own."

Sasha nodded. "You're right. I guess I don't need to worry about you two." She smiled wryly.

Wes came down to the water's edge, holding out a huge towel. "You have to watch that fair skin," he said, bundling Sasha into the towel and his arms. "You might get a bad burn. Moon burn."

Sasha tipped her head back. The clear summer sky had grown dark without her even realizing it. "But it's a new moon tonight."

"Can't be too careful," he countered, putting a fist under her chin to kiss her softly. "Let's split," he whispered, "I'd rather be alone with you."

"We have to help cook hot dogs," she murmured, burrowing her face against his hard shoulder.

"I think they can manage without us," he urged, holding her tighter.

Suddenly Sasha's eyes filled with tears. For a moment, she was back at Monticello, that day she'd gone there with her parents and Phoebe.

She'd been gazing at a portrait of Thomas Jefferson when she turned and bumped right into a stranger. Their eyes met and that was that; Sasha Jenkins and Wesley Lewis had fallen in love.

It was supposed to be forever. And now she wasn't so sure, and the feeling that something was slipping away from her, even if it wasn't as precious as she'd first thought, made her ache.

She propped her chin on Wes's shoulder to wipe discreetly at her tears, and caught sight of Rob Kendall talking to Phoebe by the campfire. Sasha found herself daydreaming about Rob, imagining long talks with him, about the book he was writing, about her job as editor of the Kennedy High paper and whether she should study journalism in college, or maybe creative writing. . . .

She blinked back to reality. "Come on," she said gently, slipping out of Wes's embrace. She took his hand. "Let's get back to the others."

Rob glanced at Sasha's profile. He hadn't been able to help witnessing the romantic scene between Sasha and Wes a few minutes ago; there might be tensions in their relationship, but they still appeared to be very involved with one another. Still, that didn't mean he, Rob, couldn't get to know her better.

"Sasha," he began.

Just then Wes called out, "Chow time, troops!" Sasha stood up and walked back to the fire with Rob, not meeting his eyes.

Everybody grabbed a plate and helped themselves to hot dogs, cole slaw, and bottles of soda that Woody had put in the river to cool. Kim pretended to be indignant when they passed up her attractively set picnic table in favor of sitting around the fire.

As Rob bit into his second hot dog with everything on it, his observant eyes scanned the group he was with. Every writer knew that body language said a lot about people and their relationships with each other. He started to play a game in his mind, deciphering the puzzle each couple there presented.

Brad and Brenda were ignoring their supper; instead they sat quietly with their arms around one another. Peter and Monica were holding hands and whispering. Chris and Ted were sitting back to back, leaning against each other. Phoebe and Michael were sitting Indian style, close but not touching; they ate and talked easily, clearly just good friends. As for Sasha and Wes . . . Rob chewed thoughtfully.

Woody had run to his car for a volleyball, even though there wasn't room for a game on the little bit of sand. "We can improvise," he said confidently.

"Sure, in the dark without a net," Ted joked.

"Since we don't have a net, Woody can stand in the middle with his arms stretched out," Kim suggested, giggling. Woody complied, and for every shot that went over the "net's" head, another was intercepted. Finally, the ball went flying out into the river.

It was Kim's fault, and she was grabbed and toted to the water's edge. Peter and Wes swung her back and forth. Kim squealed, but they showed her no mercy; into the water she went.

"Don't panic," called Woody nobly. "I'll save you!"

He dove in and even though he was a perfectly good swimmer, he made a great show of dog-paddling about, splashing and flailing. Kim threw up her hands in mock resignation and waded out herself while Woody was still clowning.

It was time to get down to business; the gang gathered again by the fire. Everyone agreed that Rob's idea about postponing the pet wash was a good one; but because of too many conflicts, they were forced to stick with the original date — that Saturday. They'd just have to work extra quick.

"Do you have any other ideas, Rob?" Chris asked.

"Well," he began, "I spoke to Mr. Bennington this afternoon." He turned to Sasha. "I told you my family is friends with his. Anyway, he said he'd be happy to let us have a spot on his cable TV station — I told him Peter and Monica would be in touch with him, since they know the most about the media."

The crowd whooped enthusiastically. Monica looked at Peter with wide eyes; he'd turned to high-five Ted.

Everybody knew Laurie Bennington's father owned the most successful cable station in the entire D.C. area. "And that's not all," Rob continued. "I don't mean just a thirty-second commercial. He suggested you put together a show of some sort. Maybe a talent show like the Follies I've heard about. And call it a 'Telethon to Save the Animals.' You can ask people to call in and pledge money for the new building."

"We could do it," Woody said thoughtfully. "Maybe we could even do excerpts from the Follies — it would take too long to put anything new together. It would still take too long to tie it in with the dog wash, if we have it this Saturday."

"Maybe not," Peter said eagerly. He gave his thick dark hair a flip. "If we could get a hold of a TV camera, somehow, we could film the pet wash as part of the show. It's asking a lot, but do you think Mr. Bennington would send over a cameraman?"

"I think he might." Rob narrowed his eyes and nodded. "He seemed really willing to contribute to such a good cause."

"What's the catch?" wondered Brenda. "It just seems to good to be true."

"No catch," Rob told her. "Just a little accommodation. Mr. Bennington wants Laurie to have a chance to be in the show if she wants."

The group exchanged wary glances. Laurie Bennington, the former terror of Kennedy High School, had really sweetened up since she began dating Dick Westergard. But she was still, with one of the most fantastic figures around and certainly the hottest wardrobe to show it off, always something of a prima donna.

"That crazy Laurie," Ted said shaking his head and smiling. "She'd insist on being the star. She'll demand an entire show written around her."

"You won't know that until you ask," Rob said mildly.

"I don't think you know Laurie very well," Peter winked at Monica. Laurie had once aspired to be Peter's partner, in and out of the radio station. Monica giggled.

Rob shrugged. "I've never met her, true. But isn't it worth it? You've got a chance to take advantage of thousands, maybe millions, of dollars of free TV time. If you're interested in raising money for the Humane Society, this is the way to go."

Sasha agreed emphatically and there were nods all around the campfire.

"Sometimes you have to think big, if you're going to get anywhere," Woody mused. "What a chance it would be for, say you, Phoebe, to sing for a huge TV audience!"

"I think I'd die of fright," Phoebe protested.

"No, you wouldn't, Pheeberooni. You sang for a live audience in the Follies, and that's much, much scarier." He kissed her fingertips with a loud smack. "You'd be bravissima!"

"Aw, pshaw." Phoebe batted her eyelashes demurely.

Rob looked at Sasha. "This would be a great chance to learn about putting together a television script." He smiled at her encouragingly and she felt her cheeks glow. Wes was silent.

Kim decided it was the perfect time to put her two cents' worth in, before she stopped to think and lost her nerve. "You know Chan Lawrence? The tennis player?"

"What about him?" Woody asked, turning to Kim with a strange look.

"Well, I was talking to him today about . . . the party we're catering at his house. And he said he'd be happy to help us out, get some publicity for our project. It sure couldn't hurt us to have somebody as well known as him on our team. What do you all think?"

Rob thought it was a good idea, and the rest of the gang agreed. Only Woody looked wary. He kept quiet as the others discussed exactly what role Chan should play.

"Maybe that camera crew could film a sequence of Chan playing tennis," Kim suggested lamely.

"Yeah, but how does that tie in to the animal shelter?" Peter asked.

"It sounds like we still need to do a lot of work if we're going to find a focus for a TV spot," said Brad. He ran a hand through his sandy hair. He caught Brenda yawning widely and laughed.

"Maybe we've talked enough business for now," said Rob. "Kim, since you're friends with Chan — " he saw that Woody stiffened slightly at his words, " — why don't the two of you work on an angle for him? For the rest of it, I think your best bet is a live telethon, right at the scene of the pet wash."

Rob continued to talk shop with Woody and Kim, tactfully avoiding any further mention of Chan Lawrence. It was obvious the tennis star was a sore subject between them. The other couples were gathering their things together and heading up the path to the parked cars.

Wes had Sasha's hand tightly gripped in his; he was more than ready to leave. "I'll see you around the Albatross, Rob," Sasha called to him as she turned to go. Rob watched her move off through the trees, dimly lit by the street lamps above.

Chapter
8

"U p and at 'em," ordered Sasha early Thursday morning, throwing a pillow across the room at Kim, who had spent the night at her house.

Kim stretched, then rolled out of bed in one easy motion. Sasha promptly snuggled back down in her own bed.

"Hey, you dirty rat, what's fair for one is fair for the other!" Kim peeled the covers off her friend. "Or are you taking the day off to lie in bed and compose poetry?"

"No way! I'm as busy and important as you are, Kimberley Barrie. I have a million things to do today!" She rolled over on her back and put her hands behind her head.

"What do you think of Rob?" she asked idly.

"Sasha Jenkins, you don't fool me for a minute! I told you before he's cute, but I also saw the way Wes reacted when Rob showed up at the beach last night. You could very well be playing with fire." Kim had already pulled on a pair of baggy khaki shorts and a turquoise T-shirt. Now she sat cross-legged on her bed and studied Sasha.

"You should know all about that," replied Sasha with a wicked grin. "Just mention the name of Chan Lawrence and Woody starts his fire-breathing dragon act. It's silly, isn't it? He should understand that Chan is merely a *business* acquaintance, right?" Sasha watched for Kim's blush and wasn't disappointed.

"Touché. My friendship with Chan is a lot like yours with Rob. I detect a certain explosive potential. Who's kidding whom?"

"Double touché." Sasha sighed, fishing for her brown terry kimono. "I'm off to take a shower because," she said with a grin, "a certain house guest preempted said shower for so long last night that a certain hostess fell asleep waiting."

"Don't give me that! *You* kept *me* up revising your feature story, making me read it over ten times."

"Well, *you* bent *my* ear all out of shape, talking half the night, trying to settle the affairs of the world. We didn't get very far, did we? We didn't even decide which of us was going to be the first woman President of the United States."

"Nope," disagreed Kim. "It'll be me. You're too romantic to be a politician."

"Okay, you win. Write your inaugural speech while I take a quick shower."

After her shower, Sasha turned her blow dryer on and quickly dried her hair. Then she closed her bedroom door so she and Kim could talk. Sasha always appreciated using Kim as a sounding board; they were both independent thinkers, but Kim had a special pragmatism that Sasha often envied. "It's crazy," she said, "but I almost wish summer were over. I have this feeling that *something's* going to happen."

"Me, too, Chicken Little. I think the sky might fall."

"In a way, reading a book and living vicariously is a lot easier than real life," Sasha said, pulling a comb through her hair. "If the suspense gets too unbearable in a book, I can always sneak a look at the last page, just to make sure everything turns out okay!"

"Wouldn't that save us so much agony," Kim mused, "if we could do the same thing in our own lives? Spy ahead to the last day of summer just to make sure we'll still be in one piece."

"Yeah, but then we'd miss all the fun, too." Sasha stepped into a pale aqua cotton jumpsuit, thought about it for a minute, and then added a white leather belt. She slipped her feet into her favorite pair of huarache sandals.

"Come with me to Camera Craft," she urged Kim. "I want your opinion on the contact prints before I show them to Mr. Miller, the editor at the *Rose Hill Bulletin* who'll be handling my article on the Humane Society and our fundraiser."

"Feed me first and I'll be happy to go," agreed Kim.

They had the kitchen to themselves because Mr. and Mrs. Jenkins had already gone to open the Albatross. Sasha passed Kim a plate of granola bars, a staple of her health-food regime.

"This is breakfast?" Kim looked doubtful. "I'm afraid my company comes a little higher-priced. You might like eating bird seed, but I don't want to risk sprouting feathers. Do you have bacon and eggs, or pancakes?"

Kim had to settle for a glass of orange juice, a bowl of whole-grain cereal, and a peach. After they'd finished breakfast, Sasha suggested they ride their bikes the long way to Camera Craft.

"Gotcha." Kim nodded conspiratorially. "You just want to happen to ride past the Benningtons' neighbors the Petersons' right? Just in case somebody's outside mowing the lawn or walking a dog."

"There's no harm in that, is there?" Sasha was trying to convince herself as much as Kim. She tucked the folder with her feature story carefully into her backpack. No, she told herself, there's no harm in hoping to run into a good friend like Rob.

Sasha saw him from half a block away and slowed her bike. Then she did a double-take. There was a white TR7 parked by the curb in front of the Petersons'; Rob wasn't alone. Sasha caught a glimpse of long blond hair and long slender legs.

She and Kim pedaled like mad, hoping to shoot by without being seen, but no such luck.

Rob looked up from pulling a suitcase from the white car's trunk just in time to wave as the two cyclists sailed by.

Sasha resisted the urge to look back over her shoulder, concentrating instead on Kim's swiftly pumping legs in front of her. Suddenly the conversation she'd had with Rob a few days earlier in the Albatross came rushing back to her. He might not make the pet wash on Saturday, even though he was more than happy to act as an advisor, because he had a "friend" coming for the weekend.

Sasha fought back the wave of disappointment that threatened to knock her off her bicycle. It was ridiculous, really. She'd just met Rob, and they were fast becoming friends, but that was all. There was no reason why they couldn't continue to chat at the bookstore, just because he had a girl friend, probably a classmate of his at St. John's. Of course he had better things to do on a summer Saturday than shampoo dogs and cats with a bunch of high school kids!

And besides, Sasha thought, as she pulled her bike up next to Kim's in front of the camera store, I have Wes. We may have differences, but he loves me. I know we'll work them out. But why do I feel so rotten?

Kim put a sympathetic arm around Sasha's shoulder without speaking.

"You saw her, too, huh?" She forced a laugh. "Maybe it's a good thing. Rob isn't really interested in me. I was just fantasizing because he's a writer and a book lover like me. Now you're the only one with a love problem, Kimberley."

"Are you giving up that easily?" asked Kim, locking her bike. "You two could have so much to offer each other."

"As friends, sure," said Sasha. "That's all it's meant to be. I was fooling myself to think for even a minute that I really had anything in common with a college man." She kept her voice light, but she suddenly felt tired. She felt like she'd looked at the last page of a love story, and while the ending wasn't exactly unhappy, it just wasn't quite right.

Kim followed Sasha inside. The man behind the counter greeted Sasha with a broad smile. Her contacts were ready: He'd get them from the back of the store.

He returned and spread the sheet on an illuminated viewing table. Kim looked over Sasha's shoulder. Printed there were rows of tiny black-and-white pictures, a whole roll of film on one glossy page. "They're small," Sasha explained, "but clear enough so that I can pick out the shots I want and discard the rest. This saves time and money."

Sasha gave the sheet a professional glance. She was pleased, a few of the photographs were very good. They brought back to her very vividly the emotions she'd felt at the Humane Society. She hoped they'd affect her readers the same way.

"Oh, look at that one," whispered Kim. "Look at those adorable kittens bundled up in that woman's arms."

"They're really quite good, Sasha," the man said. "Good composition, but most important, you manage to capture emotion. You could have a future in photo journalism."

"Oh, thank you, Mr. Fisk." Sasha was glowing again. "I'll come back when — and if — the newspaper decides on any of them. Then you can run off the prints."

"They'll want at least one," he assured her, smiling.

"I'll see you later — I hope!"

The next stop was a long, low fieldstone building, home of the *Rose Hill Bulletin*, a daily newspaper. Sasha had been here once before for an open house with the staff of the Kennedy High School paper *The Red and the Gold*, of which she was now the editor-in-chief.

Kim accompanied Sasha into the lobby; her mother and Earthly Delights didn't need her until around noon. "I want to make sure your article makes the front page, with a headline at least two inches high!"

Sasha told the receptionist she had an appointment to see Mr. Miller, the managing editor. After signing a visitor's sheet, the two girls were pointed down the hall to a glass-doored office.

Mr. Miller, in a suit and tie, contrasted with the other employees Sasha and Kim had glimpsed. The newspaper office seemed to be a casual place for the most part.

"Hello there," he said, standing up to greet them with a smile. "Let's see what you've got."

Sasha handed him the manila envelope and the contact sheets. He checked the pictures first, studying them silently for so long that Sasha got butterflies. She and Kim exchanged an apprehensive look.

Then Mr. Miller nodded. "These are excellent," he said, putting the contact sheet aside and turning to the four neatly typed pages.

Sasha felt like she was back in school with her

fingers crossed, hoping the faculty advisor would give her thumbs-up on a story for *The Red and the Gold*.

Right now, Sasha's hands were clammy. It was one thing to write for high school kids; this was the real world. She'd die if Mr. Miller laughed at her childish attempts. Kim patted her knee sympathetically.

He read through her article quickly even though it seemed like forever to Sasha. When he looked up, he smiled.

"It's good," he said. "Too long, but good. The rule of thumb is, if you can't say it in one page, it isn't worth saying. However, for an important feature, we sometimes go two or even three pages."

Sasha was holding her breath. Would he use the story or wouldn't he? It would break her heart, but she'd cut it to half a page if she had to.

Mr. Miller turned back to the contact sheet. He circled one of the pictures, the shot of the first puppy Sasha had fallen in love with, looking longingly through the chain fence, straight into the viewer's heart.

"You take this out to the City Room," Mr. Miller said, handing the article to her. "Give it to Elaine Black, the Lifestyles Editor. I'll mark it up for tomorrow, so you'll have to hurry and get that glossy print made up."

Kim couldn't contain herself; she jumped to her feet and threw her arms around Sasha.

Sasha wanted to whoop with joy. "Oh, thank you, Mr. Miller," she said, her big brown eyes glowing.

"One other thing," he said thoughtfully. "I think the paper can help in another way. One of your objectives is to find homes for those animals, isn't it?"

Sasha and Kim nodded.

"I think we can try running a Pet of the Week picture on a regular basis, along with a brief description of the animal in need of a home. Could you handle the pictures and the information?"

Now Sasha felt like turning cartwheels. She could hardly believe their luck. They'd come up with the idea of a pet wash just to call attention to the needs of the animal shelter and look what was happening!

She thanked Mr. Miller again, and with Kim in tow, headed for the City Room, about an acre of open space crammed with desks, where they found the Lifestyles Editor over by a window.

Elaine was wearing a headset and talking into a small mouthpiece, typing on a computer terminal at the same time.

She held up a finger, smiling at Sasha and Kim, and pointed to a chair beside her desk. Kim gestured for Sasha to sit. "Editor for a day," she whispered.

Elaine switched off her headphones and held out a hand for Sasha's copy.

"I should hang by the thumbs for this," she said, with another smile, waving to an almost completed page dummy on her desk. Sasha could see the ads blocked in among the pictures and stories. "What have you got here? Mr. Miller just gave me the orders to get this in ASAP." She ran an eye over the picture and the article.

"We'll give it space, maybe a two-column cut, but you're going to have to run like a gazelle and get me the print."

Kim broke in. "I could bike back to the camera shop," she volunteered. "You stay here, Sash."

Sasha looked up to answer Kim, glancing over at the City Editor's desk as she did so. She caught a glimpse of a familiar sandy-haired head. Her heart was already racing with the thrill of almost being a big-time journalist; it broke the world's record now. What could Rob Kendall be doing here?

Elaine was already on the phone with the camera shop, arranging to have number five from Sasha's contact sheet printed immediately. Kim was tying her shoes, getting ready to sprint for her bike.

Sasha felt light-headed; the bright lights, the success of her feature, the clatter of typewriters, Rob . . . it was all so overwhelming. She realized she was still staring across the crowded room at the back of Rob's head when he turned around and suddenly she found herself looking right into his eyes. His face lit up with pleased recognition and he smiled. Even from this far away, Sasha could see the one dimple in his left cheek that gave her goose bumps.

Chapter
9

Rob started to weave his way among the desks in their direction. It was too late to take off for Camera Craft; she couldn't pretend she hadn't seen him. Sasha looked around hopefully for another avenue of escape, but short of ducking under the Lifestyles Editor's desk, she was trapped.

Kim had noticed Sasha's distress and now gave her hand a supportive squeeze. "Hang in there, kid," she whispered. "Keep your cool. Show him you have as much self-possession as any college girl."

"Right," Sasha said, lifting her chin. There was absolutely no reason to make a fool of herself. And anyway, what do I have to be afraid of? Sasha asked herself. It's not as if anything embarrassing has ever happened between us. If I had a little crush on him, it was my secret; he couldn't possibly know how I felt. I didn't even know how I felt!

Maybe that's exactly the problem, Sasha realized. I'm not afraid of Rob, I'm afraid of myself.

"Hi, Sasha. Hi, Kim," Rob called out cheerfully. "What are nice girls like you doing in a place like this?" He winked at Sasha and touched her lightly on the shoulder, then went around to the other side of the desk.

"How's it going, Elaine?" he asked.

"Hi, Rob." She smiled at him. Kim raised her eyebrows at Sasha. What's the story? she asked silently. Sasha could only shrug.

Rob handed Elaine a sheet of typing paper. "The Rose Hill Date Book," he said with a grin, glancing at the wall clock. "A full half hour before deadline."

Elaine rolled her eyes and laughed. "What a guy, Rob." She spread a blank page dummy out on her desk, and with a ruler began blocking in a new page composition to include Sasha's story. Elaine obviously didn't need her anymore; now was her chance to make a getaway. It would be a relief not to have to converse with Rob, but at the same time Sasha was curious, both personally and professionally, about what Rob was doing at the *Bulletin*.

"Are you two leaving?" Rob asked. "So am I. Let me walk you outside."

"Rob, what brings you here?" Kim had read Sasha's mind and put the question to him, which was lucky for Sasha. Her tongue seemed to have frozen to the roof of her mouth.

"I'm a stringer," Rob explained. "I dig up tidbits about Rose Hill — a little neighborhood news, some historical trivia, a human interest-type story — anything I can get my hands on. I submit them for the Date Book, and get paid by the column inch. It's a good deal — I'm polishing my research and journalistic techniques and having some fun at the same time."

"I thought you were writing a book," Sasha said, astonished. "When do you have time for it? With this, and your social life, I mean, and everything else." She couldn't help noticing that Rob looked especially gorgeous in a pair of charcoal gray trousers and a white Oxford shirt.

His sleeves were pushed up over his browned, nicely muscled forearms; he gestured as he spoke. Sasha liked people who talked with their hands — it was a sign of a lively, creative mind. She couldn't help inwardly comparing Rob's warm, open manner with Wes's reserved, controlled style. The only gesture he ran to was the salute.

"My social life?" Rob laughed. "It's not exactly a full-time job. I have some friends in the area, but most of my college buddies are scattered for the summer."

Sasha bit her tongue. She wanted to ask about the blond girl, but she knew she didn't have a right to pry. Kim caught her eye. She mouthed the words, Should I? Sasha shook her head.

"And let me tell you something about writing a book," Rob said as he steered them through the reception area. He held the heavy glass doors open. "How about having lunch?" He looked from Sasha to Kim and back again.

Kim couldn't apologize fast enough for having

97

to run home that instant; she had menus to plan, cookbooks to read, phone calls to make, dishes to wash, you name it.

"Thanks anyway!" she called back. "See you guys around."

Sasha turned to Rob to make her own excuses. "I really should get to the camera shop to pick up that print. . . ." She knew she didn't sound very convincing. Rob held her eyes steadily; she knew she didn't look convincing.

"It can't possibly be ready yet," he assured her. "Having lunch with me is the perfect way to kill time until it is." He was smiling at her: cool, friendly, just right. There was no hint of an intimacy that shouldn't be there.

Sasha nodded. "Okay. That sounds good."

"What do you think?" Rob was glancing up and down the street. "How about the sub shop? I've never been there." He opened the door on the passenger side of his car for her.

"Oh, it's fun," said Sasha. "I go there all the time with my friends."

Inside the sub shop, Sasha led Rob to one of the booths in the back. Even in the middle of the day, the pleasantly cluttered restaurant was dimly lit. Rob was amused by the cigar store Indian, the old motorcycle on the wall. It was a comfortable place and practically a second home to Sasha and all her gang, but she didn't feel particularly comfortable now. It was strange to be there with Rob instead of Woody and Kim, or Phoebe . . . or Wes. Somehow in this environment he seemed even older, more of an outsider. And it wasn't like being in the Albatross, chatting up a storm about poetry and history and drama. She had no books now to hide behind.

They ordered sandwiches and sodas, and then Sasha propped her elbows on the table, chin in hands. She was determined to seem casual and it was exciting to have a chance to talk more to Rob — just the two of them.

"All right, tell me more about your book. How come you have time to do everything in the world except write it?"

Rob grinned at her. "I've fallen into a trap," he said. "I always thought that if I just had enough time, I'd spend it writing until all of a sudden, I'd have three hundred pages of manuscript, ready for the publisher."

"Then why don't you do it?" Sasha asked. "You have the chance this summer."

He laughed, his hazel eyes crinkling closed. Sasha's heart skipped a beat and she looked down into her glass of natural cream soda.

"I was a fool to think it would just happen that way. The other day I read something about a woman writer who discovered she had the neatest house in town, even though she *hated* housework. Even her closets were neat! She finally realized she was rationalizing like crazy, telling herself the housework always had to be done first because it was so hard to force herself to sit down at the typewriter."

"So you're rationalizing," Sasha nodded. "You're a stringer at the *Bulletin*; you've read practically every book in stock at the Albatross; I bet your closet is spotless!" Sasha was laughing but her warm brown eyes conveyed her sympathy.

"Something like that," Rob admitted.

Rob rolled his eyes and shook his head, laughing. "You just don't know," he began, but before he could continue somebody slid onto the bench beside him. It was the blond girl from this morning, and she was just as beautiful as Sasha could have imagined. Sasha felt her face fall; she struggled to assume a neutral expression.

She'd forgotten all about the girl and her suitcase and her car; Rob had made her forget. She should have known they weren't likely to disappear.

The girl placed a proprietary hand on Rob's arm.

"I thought I might find you here," she said. He was smiling at her. Now she turned and looked at Sasha inquiringly.

"Sasha, this is Cathy Silver. Cath, Sasha Jenkins. Her mom and dad own that bookstore I was telling you about."

Cathy extended a hand, with a friendly smile. "It's nice to meet you," she said.

Sasha shook her hand with as bright a smile as she could muster, then she glanced at her watch. "Oh, I really have to run, I'm really late picking up that print! Nice seeing you, Rob. Bye, Cathy!"

All in one movement Sasha was up and out of the booth, reaching in the pocket of her jumpsuit for a few dollars to pay for her sandwich and practically tossing it on the table, heading for the door.

"See you around, Sasha. Congratulations again on that article," Rob called after her.

I will not have tears in my eyes, Sasha told herself firmly as she raced through the sub shop. I'm not a baby. Rob has never implied that he thinks about me as anything other than a friend. It wouldn't be right if he did; I have Wes, don't I? I have Wes.

Sasha crashed full force into somebody just as she reached the door of the sub shop. Woody Webster wrapped his arms around her.

"Steady," he whispered. "The enemy is watching. They know you have the documents. The blond woman works for the Kremlin. She's licensed to kill."

Sasha couldn't resist a giggle.

In a louder voice, he said, "Let's go get a pizza. This place looks sort of crowded."

They piled out on the sidewalk laughing. "I just may have saved your life," Woody said seriously. "No really, Kim sent me, on my half day off from the theater, mind you, to ask you if by any chance you accepted a ride to lunch and left your bike at the newspaper. I don't pretend to understand any of this — she assured me it was just women's intuition."

Sasha laughed ruefully. "Good call, Kim! Ol' head-in-the-clouds Jenkins does it again."

"And your pal Woody just happens to have a bike rack on the back of his Volvo," he said.

Woody took Sasha to pick up the glossy first; they turned it in to Elaine and then retrieved the bike. He suggested taking a spin on their way home and since Sasha wasn't in a hurry — she had some paperwork to do at the Albatross but it could wait — she was happy to go for a ride.

"Kim sounds like she's pretty busy these days with the Lawrences' party," Sasha said, keeping her voice neutral. "Hey Woody, thanks again for coming to my rescue. You're a real friend."

"Any time, Sasha. I know you'd do the same for me." Woody was staring straight ahead; it occurred to Sasha that considering he'd suggested a scenic drive, he wasn't seeing much of the scenery. Both his hands were gripped tightly on the steering wheel and his forehead was creased in a very un-Woody-like frown. Sasha opened her mouth to ask, "Is something bothering you, Woody?" just as he said, "Sasha — "

"Yes, Woody?"

"Sash, I . . . it's Kim. It's Kim and me." Sasha's heart melted at the pain she heard in Woody's voice. "Sasha, do you think that Kim doesn't . . . that Kim would rather she and I were more like me and you — I mean, just good friends?"

His voice was husky, and when he turned to look quickly at her, Sasha saw that his eyes were wet.

"Oh, Woody. Did Kim tell you that?"

"She doesn't have to tell me," he said, pounding the palm of one hand lightly on the wheel. He took a deep breath. "All I had to do was look at her, all I had to do was see the way she looked at Chan Lawrence that first day we went to his house, the way she talks about him. I can't compete with a guy like that. I can just tell, Sash. Kim doesn't have to say anything. I can tell when we're together — things just aren't the same."

The words tumbled out; Woody's face reddened. Sasha knew how difficult it must be for him to confess his feelings to her like this. He had pulled the car over onto the grass beside the road; now he cut off the engine and the two sat in silence for a moment. Sasha searched her mind for something to say that could make Woody feel better, but something that wasn't a lie.

"You and Kim are different in some ways," Sasha said, "you know that. You have to remember how important it is to her that you two keep a sense of your own selves, outside of your relationship."

Woody was silent. He ran one hand through his thick red hair and sighed. He gave Sasha a very weak smile.

"The party is on Friday," she said with a confidence she didn't feel, "and by Saturday it'll all be over."

The minute she spoke them, Sasha wished she could take the words back. Kim had told her she was attracted to Chan. Maybe she was all wrong to talk so optimistically.

Woody had started the car. They were heading back toward Rose Hill.

"I never had a girl friend before," Woody said, suddenly.

"We're all beginners when it comes to love," Sasha pointed out. "There're bound to be some rough edges."

Sasha realized she could just as well be talking about herself — and Wes. Wes was *her* first love. They too were having some problems now. Maybe she was trying to reassure herself.

"When you've got a good thing, you just don't throw it away," she said aloud.

Chapter
10

"What are you going to do if it rains on Chan's party?" asked Sasha with a wicked smile.

She had stopped off at Kim's house on Friday morning because she didn't have to be at work until eleven and found herself shanghaied into helping construct a watermelon whale. The two girls were working at the wider butcher block counter in the Barries' spacious kitchen.

"Don't say such a thing. Don't even think it," Kim answered, shaking her melon ball scoop at Sasha. "The weatherman wouldn't dare."

"Consider me chastened," said Sasha. "I should have known you and your mom wouldn't let a little detail like that slip by you."

"Well, we reserved a tent just in case, but my fingers are crossed. A barbecue under a tent just wouldn't be the same thing."

Kim looked out the window for the hundredth time. The sky was overcast but the sun was trying to break through.

"Hey, wait a minute!" she exclaimed. Sasha was making a blind stab at the watermelon. "Give me that knife before you slit your wrist and bleed all over the centerpiece for the party."

"If I'm willing to give my life's blood for the cause, you should be grateful." Sasha laughed, giving up the knife gladly.

"Now watch this," said Kim in a professional tone. "It's easy."

Sasha stepped back dubiously. Kim eyed the watermelon for a moment, then went to work.

She cut the top off the melon, leaving a saw-tooth edge; then she carved out the entire luscious, red center, halved it, and handed Sasha a melon ball scoop.

"Here, you do this part. I think you can manage it without killing yourself." She demonstrated how to cut one neat little ball of melon, removing the seeds as you went along.

"You're a real pro," Sasha said admiringly. "I guess that's why you're a chef and I'm a poet, huh?"

"Right," said Kim. While Sasha laboriously scooped at the seemingly endless mountain of watermelon, Kim briskly halved a cantaloupe and then a honeydew melon, scooping out the seeds and filling a bowl with tiny pale peach and green balls of melon.

She glanced at Sasha, who'd shifted her grip on the melon scoop. "Come on, hup! Hup! I thought you were an artist — this should be right up your alley."

"I said I was a poet, not a sculptor!" Sasha burst into giggles. Kim, in her mad dash through the melons, had managed to sprinkle her smooth short hair liberally with seeds.

Kim turned back to the hollowed-out watermelon. She closed one eye and held an index finger out in front of her nose. Sasha giggled again. Picking up the knife, she cut a huge, gaping mouth in the watermelon shell and stuck some seeds in for teeth, then she stood back again.

"What do you think?"

"Vicious," said Sasha. "Most definitely a man-eater." Kim reached for two stuffed olives to use as eyes, turning them so the poor whale was crossed-eyed.

"I don't know," said Sasha. "That kind of diminishes the killer effect."

Kim rotated the olives so the whale was gazing upward. Sasha shrieked with laughter. "He's saying, 'Can you believe what I have to put up with?' "

The melon taken care of, the two girls wiped the counter clean of seeds and juice. Kim carefully wrapped the whale and stored him in the huge refrigerator.

"What's next?" asked Sasha.

"What's next. . . ." Kim's eyes darted rapidly around the kitchen. "Oh, gosh, there are so many things still left to do, I don't know where to start, and we have to go over there to set up in two hours!" Kim suddenly felt paralyzed, the soles of her bare feet one substance with the tiles of the kitchen floor. Suddenly she wished the party was going to be anywhere but the Lawrences'. What if something went wrong, what if she looked like a fool in front of Chan? What if *something* went right, between the two of them?

She turned wide green eyes to Sasha. "Help!"

Sasha read her like a book. "Are you nervous about seeing Chan again? I know it must make you feel so mixed up, I mean finding him so attractive when you're in love with someone else." Sasha hadn't told Kim about her conversation with Woody; he hadn't asked her to intercede and she respected his confidence.

"I envy you," Kim said. "You were in the same boat, wondering how come you were so interested in Rob, if that meant that maybe Wes wasn't right for you. And your problem was solved for you."

"Maybe you'll find out tonight that Chan has something going with another girl. Would that make you feel any better?"

Kim sighed, her eyes miserable. "No," she said softly.

Sasha put a comforting arm around her.

"I wish I'd never laid eyes on Chan Lawrence!" Kim burst out, suddenly. She flung Sasha's arm off and stomped around the kitchen. "Woody and I were perfectly happy until he came along."

She stopped stomping and sat down defeatedly on one of the stools by the counter. "Oh, Sasha," she said, her voice breaking. "If I'm able even to feel something for someone else — anyone else — even if nothing comes of it, does that mean that what Woody and I have isn't real?"

"I don't know, Kimmie," Sasha said, her own eyes filled with tears. "I just don't know the answer."

A few minutes later Mrs. Barrie blew into the kitchen like a whirlwind. She tossed the keys to her wagon to Kim.

"I had a bit of luck, sweetheart," she said, pulling open the door to the freezer and peering inside.

"I ran into Woody on my way to the party rental place — he helped me load the picnic tables and barbecue. He's out in the car now. He'll go with you to the Lawrences' to help set up, and that will free me up to get to work here."

Kim's heart sank right down to her heels. She'd only just finished drying her eyes. The last thing she wanted in the whole world was to see Woody, much less have him with her when she saw Chan.

"Come with me!" she whispered to Sasha. "You can keep Woody busy, make it look like he's *your* boyfriend."

"That would be wrong," Sasha whispered back.

"But you'll come anyway, just for support?"

Sasha hesitated, but she couldn't resist the pleading in her friend's eyes. "I'm not crazy about being the *fifth wheel* in this scheme, but I'll go." Kim squeezed her hand gratefully.

Woody leaped out of the station wagon the instant Kim and Sasha appeared at the door. He wrapped his arms around Kim in a welcoming hug, and Kim found herself trying with all her might to respond the way she used to, with the same joy and enthusiasm. But even though Woody's arms around her felt natural, as warm and caring as ever, she couldn't help thinking about Chan.

She could tell Woody was hurt by her reception. "Don't pay any attention to me," she excused herself lamely. "I'm just tense about the party. I'm so afraid something will go wrong."

He assisted her tenderly into the passenger seat and gave her another kiss on the nose. "Don't worry about a thing. I'm going to be right there with you, your number one troubleshooter."

"Not tonight at the party, though," she reminded him.

"Now, tonight; any time my girl needs help," he said, opening Sasha's door for her, then sliding in behind the wheel. "I'll always be there for you, always."

Kim felt awful. Just when she was knee-deep in traitorous thoughts about Chan Lawrence, he had to be so wonderful, so, so Woody — just to underline the fact that she didn't come close to deserving a guy as special as him.

Kim was quiet as the three headed toward Park Heights in the Barries' station wagon. Sasha did a good imitation of a chatterbox just to fill up some of the silence. At one point she leaned forward to sneak a look at Woody. His face was determined; obviously he'd decided against sitting back and letting things just take their course while his heart broke. He wasn't giving up on Kim that easily.

The gates were open when they reached Wildcliff. A gardener was waiting to help them unload the tables and carry them around to the back of the house.

The party was to be in a secluded area, past the tennis courts and beyond a twelve-foot hedge that was sheared to perfection on the sides and top.

As they rounded the hedge, Sasha realized how magnificent the Lawrence estate was. Kim was scanning the grassy lawns around the pool to decide upon the location for the picnic tables and grills.

Sasha watched Woody watch Kim. He seemed to be losing some of the self-confidence she'd detected on the way over, poor guy, and Chan Lawrence hadn't even arrived at the scene yet.

To make him feel better, Sasha whispered, "This is a nice place to visit, but I wouldn't want to live here."

"Said she, crossing her fingers and toes," he murmured.

She shook her head. "No, seriously. This is all for show, to impress people. My family isn't exactly poor, but I was brought up to have different values. I don't think of myself as better than other people and I wouldn't want other people to think I think I am, if you know what a mean."

"Yeah, sure." Woody was looking in the direction of the pool house where Kim was now talking with Mrs. Lawrence.

Sasha shrugged. Well, I tried, she thought. And what can I say, it is a great place for a party.

Kim and Mrs. Lawrence, their arms linked, were strolling toward them. Sasha thought Kim looked incredibly uncomfortable; Mrs. Lawrence, however, was all smiles. She acted as if meeting Sasha was the most privileged moment of her life, and "of course" she remembered meeting Mr. Webster the other day! Kim stood by smiling weakly.

"How nice to see some of Kim's friends," said Mrs. Lawrence. "Kim is such a dear girl. We're already so fond of her. I do hope you two will come to my son's birthday party tonight. He does so want to meet Kim's friends."

Before either Woody or Kim could say something rash, Sasha spoke, clearly and firmly. "Thank you very much, Mrs. Lawrence, but Woody and I have other plans! Please extend our best wishes to your son, though!"

"Well, dear, I'll put both your names on the guest list in case you change your minds."

Sasha caught Kim's eye and read her silent thanks. I really didn't even do that for you, she wanted to say, I did it for Woody. I would never subject him to humiliation at the hands of these people.

She was ready to leave and knew Woody was, too. He had drawn completely inside of himself; his face was expressionless. When they went back to the pool house to hang a huge HAPPY 19TH BIRTHDAY, CHAN banner, Kim asked eagerly for his opinion on where exactly to place it, and how high, as if to apologize, but Woody didn't respond. He remained as stiff as the wooden Indian in the sub shop.

Just when Sasha thought they would escape without the straw that might break Woody's back — an encounter with Chan — who should stroll cooly around the hedge, brightly suited for tennis practice, than the birthday boy himself.

Chan made a beeline for Kim; he didn't even glance at Woody and Sasha. So much for being *so eager* to meet Kim's friends! Sasha thought grimly. She didn't think she had ever seen Woody so tense, and when Chan slung his arm lightly across Kim's shoulders as they walked about the pool area discussing the party setup, she was sure he was going to explode momentarily. Instead, he stuffed his fists deep into his pockets.

"I'll be at the car, Kim," he said in a hoarse voice. He turned without another look in their direction and strode up the path back toward the courts and the house. Sasha was torn; she wanted to tear Kim away from Chan, but she also wanted Woody to know she was on his side. And when she saw Kim's face as she talked to Chan — oblivious to what had just happened with Woody — she was suddenly so angry with her that she didn't trust herself not to say something she might regret.

"We'll wait in the car," Sasha said.

Kim acknowledged her with a wave. "I'll only be a minute more."

The car ride back was a nightmare. Sasha could hardly breathe, there were so many angry and unhappy vibrations pressing on her. Kim was driving and when she pulled up at Woody's house, he got out of the car without a word.

The two girls drove on in painful silence.

Sasha wanted to tell Kim honestly that she thought she'd behaved abominably to Woody, but when she saw the tears rolling down Kim's cheeks, she softened.

"I'm so ashamed of myself, Sasha."

"Oh, Kim."

"I don't know what's wrong with me," Kim

sniffled. "I hate myself, but I can't help myself. I feel like I'm losing control of my own life."

Sasha patted her arm sympathetically.

Kim shook her head. "It's so weird. I like having him, Chan, pay attention to me. When he looks at me, I can't think about anything else. He put his arm around me and it was like Woody never existed."

Tears welled up in her eyes again. "But I still love Woody, I do, and I could kill myself for making him hurt. But Sasha, I just don't know if what I want is to kiss and make up with him, try to pretend things are just the way they used to be, because they aren't. I'm not."

"I don't know what to say, Kim," Sasha sighed. "I love you and I love Woody, I'd like you both to be happy. But you're the only one who can figure out your feelings."

"What if I never do?"

"Oh, you will. It might just take time."

Kim had pulled up in front of the Albatross. Sasha leaned over and gave her a big hug. "Good luck, my friend."

"Bye, Sash."

Back home, Kim ran up the stairs to splash her face with cold water. She patted it dry. All signs of tears were just about erased. There was no point in looking hysterical in front of her mom; she didn't want her to think she couldn't handle the responsibility of helping out with the Lawrences' party.

"Hey, Mom," she said brightly as she entered the kitchen. "Making progress?"

"I think we're right on schedule — do you

want to take over with this garlic bread?" Kim grabbed a knife and set to work, slicing the homemade loaves on the diagonal, but not cutting in far enough to separate the slices. She spread the bread with butter and pressed garlic, wrapped it in aluminum foil, and briefed her mother on how things had gone at the Lawrences' setting up for the barbecue.

Mrs. Barrie listened in silence until Kim's voice trailed off, then put down her own knife to look at her daughter. "Am I right in thinking there's more here than meets the eye?"

"You could always read me like a book," Kim answered with a wry smile.

"Want to talk about it?"

"We don't have time — there's still so much to do to get ready."

"You're more important to me than a hundred birthday barbecues," Mrs. Barrie said, leaning forward to wipe a smear of garlic butter from Kim's cheek. "If there ever comes a day when I don't have time to talk with you, I'll give up the catering business." She held out her arms.

Kim hugged her mother tightly, her eyes stinging with tears. She knew how lucky she was to have been born into this particular family. It wasn't always easy, having to move every couple of years, leaving friends behind, going to a new school. But where it really mattered, right inside her family, she had all the love and security anyone could ask for.

"It's Woody, isn't it?" Mrs. Barrie said gently, stroking her daughter's hair.

"Sort of," Kim hiccupped. "I love him. I guess

114

he's just about the nicest person I've ever met, aside from you and Dad. But now, since I met Chan the other day, I have so many mixed-up feelings. I don't even know if Chan's really interested in me. It's all crazy. Why don't I appreciate what I've got with Woody?"

Mrs. Barrie took a step back from Kim and put her hands on her shoulders, looking her in the eyes.

"You do appreciate Woody," she said carefully. "But sometimes in life things can seem completely confused. And often, when you don't know what to do, the best thing to do is nothing at all. It can be a mistake to force things when you aren't clear about your real objectives."

"I thought the best thing was always to face your problems head on." Kim turned to lean against the counter.

"That's the first rule of thumb, but you can't always generalize. Flexibility is a must. Honey, does that help at all?"

Kim sighed. "Yeah, it helps," she said. She picked up the knife and pretended to inspect the sharpness of the blade. She still felt dangerously close to tears. "Hey, Mom, we'd better get cracking."

"Right, partner." Mrs. Barrie gave her daughter a squeeze and Kim smiled warily.

"We're going to knock 'em dead tonight, huh, Mom?"

"You bet. We're some caterers."

Chapter
11

By evening, Sasha had decided to go to the Lawrences' party after all. She'd called Kim from the bookstore to give her a final word of support and realized that maybe something more than words was called for.

"Do you want me to beg you to come?" Kim had said. "I'll beg you. Please, Sash."

Mrs. Barrie had taken the phone from Kim and spoken to Sasha herself. "We could use an extra hand, if you want to know the truth. How would you like to join the Earthly Delights team?"

So it was all set: Sasha was going to help serve at the barbecue. Kim's mom even wanted to pay her, but Sasha wouldn't think of it. Now she was having second thoughts. A party was a party, it was true, but somehow she had a feeling this particular party wasn't exactly going to be a barrel of laughs.

"Then why go?" asked her father, reasonably. He was emptying the Albatross's cash register. "Nobody's holding a gun to your head."

"It's the vibes, Dad," Sasha said. She looked up from dusting and straightening the New Arrivals section. "I keep feeling like Kim is sending me calls for help and I know she's counting on me. The people who are going to be at this party — tennis bums or whatever they are — they're not people Kim knows anything about. She just doesn't think she's ready to face Chan's friends on her own."

Mr. Jenkins locked the cash register. "You know what's right, baby."

Sasha took a clean dust rag from her mother, who'd just emerged from the back office with an armful of books to shelve. "Thanks, Mom. Yeah, Kim needs a backup and I'm it, even if I'd rather ride the tumbrel to the guillotine."

She struck a pose: Sidney Carton, *A Tale of Two Cities.*

" 'It is a far, far better thing I do than ever I have done,' " she quoted dramatically.

Her father laughed, picked up a pair of scissors, and made a swiping motion. "Off with her head!"

Mrs. Jenkins tossed over her car keys. "Take the VW. It'll be more comfortable than the tumbrel at least."

"Thank you, Madame de Farge. I trust you'll have my shroud knitted by the time my head rolls."

Her mother smiled ruefully. "I apologize for this, but I can't resist telling you to get a move on, you little Dickens."

Mr. Jenkins howled and Sasha giggled helplessly. This was exactly why she was apprehensive about the party at Chan's. She could carry on serious or silly conversations with her mom and dad, with the bookstore regulars, with Rob Kendall — right from the moment they met — with the kids at Kennedy High. But she couldn't imagine what she could possibly have in common with the tennis star and his friends.

Not that she'd expected them to quote Dickens, but they probably wouldn't even know what she was talking about if she tried to break the ice by discussing the latest best-seller. She'd seen the library in Wildcliff. It had bookshelves, but they didn't hold books. They were stuffed with trophies. The closest thing to a book she could see was a copy of *Tennis World* magazine.

Some library! It was practically wallpapered with big, framed pictures, every last one of them of Chan: Chan shaking hands with Jimmy Connors, with Ivan Lendl, with John McEnroe. There was a big screen with a VCR and Sasha presumed that every single cassette was action footage of guess who.

Back at her house to change, Sasha couldn't help getting just a little bit excited. Any of their other friends would be jealous if they knew she was going. Except maybe Woody. She swallowed a tiny bit of guilt as she fussed with the sash of her new, deep rose, drop-waisted minidress. Would Woody think she was selling out? There: Now the full, soft folds were hanging just right. No, in his heart of hearts, Woody wanted what was best for Kim, and what was best for Kim was for Sasha to go with her to the Lawrences'.

Sasha eyed her reflection with approval; the dress's slightly wide shoulders and bloused top were becoming. She glanced at the clock and picked up her pace. She brushed her hair quickly, grabbed her bag, and as an afterthought stuffed a paperback in it. "Just in case I end up sitting by myself in the library!"

There were half a dozen bottles of champagne chilling in buckets and every type of soda imaginable.

Kim couldn't help but be delighted. What a wonderful backdrop for a very special Barrie-catered party! Colorful Japanese lanterns strung from the trees cast a soft glow; the pool was lit by underwater lights that made the mosaic fish leap and dance. Just then there was a burst of music, apparently piped down from the house.

People began drifting across the lawn in twos and threes, all of them very tanned, and very well dressed. The party had begun.

Kim stood mesmerized, watching the guests come down the grassy hill, disappear briefly behind the hedge, then reappear by the pool. Her feet were rooted to the redwood deck; she hardly even noticed that her mother and Sasha had moved off toward the picnic tables to oversee the buffet.

So many blond heads! So many older-looking girls in beautiful, boldly flowered summer party dresses, so many gorgeous guys who looked as if they could easily be tennis stars, too. Kim looked down at her own outfit, so carefully chosen earlier that evening. Suddenly peach-colored silk parachute pants ("Silk to a barbecue?" Mrs. Barrie had said in despair) and a loose white T-shirt deeply V-ed in the back didn't seem quite the thing.

Kim had a sudden urge to run and hide behind the watermelon whale, but then she saw Chan walking toward her with a group of friends in tow. She felt frozen; her heart stopped and then started up again at twice its normal rate as those so-blue eyes, the bright hair, the wide welcoming smile came up close.

When Chan kissed her lightly on the cheek, she almost fainted. Any fears she might have had that Chan would introduce one of the beautiful girls with him — could that be *the* Cassie? — as his girl friend dissolved when he said to his friends, "Folks, this is Kim. She and her mom are catering this bash. Wait'll you taste her cooking!"

His friends laughed, but at Chan, not at her. Kim felt herself begin to relax. Chan had spoken lightly, not making a big deal out of the fact that she was the hired help tonight, but rather introducing her as a friend.

A very good friend. "So everybody be really nice to her. Hey, guys, don't get any ideas! She's not dancing with anyone but me!"

Kim caught a flash of jealousy in one girl's eye — a dark, striking, very red-lipped brunette that *had* to be Cassie! But before she would wonder any further, Chan had drawn her away from the rest of the talking, laughing group.

"It means a lot to me to have you here tonight, Kim," he said, his voice deep with sincerity. He put a hand on her arm and she felt the electricity shoot up to her shoulder. "We've only just met, but I already feel as if I know you really well. You know, a nice natural girl like you — you really stand out in this crowd. You've got class. I think you could be very good for me."

Chan's face was so close to hers that Kim was almost certain he was going to kiss her again, and not on the cheek. And she had a feeling she wouldn't push him away. But suddenly out of the corner of her eye she saw Sasha walk by with an elegantly arranged tray of hors d'oeuvres.

Kim pulled away with a start. How rude of her to stand and chat with Chan and his friends while her mother and Sasha did all the work! "Chan, I have to go help my mom. I — "

He put a finger to her lips. "I'll be enjoying myself, but not as much as I would if you could stay with me. Don't work too hard, Kim." He gave her another high-voltage smile and then turned to join a group of kids standing at the bar, tall frosty glasses of fruity, whipped drinks in hand.

Kim walked on air over to the picnic tables, where her mother was garnishing two large bowls of cold pasta salad with parsley. Mrs. Barrie gave her a quick, understanding glance. "Kim, dear, go check on the barbecue. I think we're ready to put the first round of steaks on."

Kim carried a platter of raw steaks over to the barbecue. The delicious smell of roasting corn filled her nostrils. She felt a twinge of pride; Earthly Delights knew how to do things right.

The next few hours passed in a blur. Even with the help of the extra people the Lawrences had hired, Sasha, Kim, and Mrs. Barrie were kept hopping, from carving steaks to slicing the steaming homemade pies bursting with apples, cherries, or peaches.

Kim worked effortlessly, though. Every few minutes she'd glance out into the crowd and meet Chan's eyes and that was all she needed to feel infused with new energy. And she didn't spill a single drop on her silk pants!

Even Sasha seemed to be enjoying herself, which made Kim feel a little less guilty about dragging her along, now that it looked like she'd had no reason to worry about anything — the party, Chan, his friends.

Sasha was chatting brightly with the guests as she served. When Kim gave her a platter to refill with steaks and corn from the grill, a tall, tow-headed boy took it out of her hands.

"Hey, let me get that for you," he said, winking one green eye.

"You're a guest," she said with a smile. "Go party."

"I'm not a cook," he laughed. "Put me in a kitchen and I'm lost, but outdoors, I'm a Boy Scout."

Sasha put her mouth close to Kim's ear and whispered, "Some of these people aren't as snobby as I expected. Some of them are even nice!" When the tow-headed boy returned with an overflowing platter, Sasha introduced herself.

"I'm Brent," he said, "and that's Craig and

122

Claire and Trip and Lance." He waved the corn tongs in their direction.

"Are you on the tennis circuit with Chan?" Sasha asked, taking the tongs from him and steering him back around to the front of the buffet table.

"Sure, I play," he said. "I'm not quite in Chan's league, but we practice together pretty often at the Club. Those four, though, aren't players — they're Clubbers." They all laughed.

"Hey, Brent." A few more tanned, husky guys had joined the group by the buffet. "Did someone say this little girl is interested in some coaching sessions?"

"Don't listen to them," teased Brent. "They're talking about moonlight sessions. Quite different from playing during the day."

Sasha smiled and blushed, shooting a glance at Kim. The two girls turned to lift another big bowl of fruit salad onto the table. "I think moonlight sessions sound like fun," Kim said, giggling.

Sasha rolled her eyes. "These tennis players and their groupies are a smooth crowd. It looks like they really know how to make the moves."

Kim shrugged. "Well, I like them. I think they're very nice."

They were just about finished serving supper, the last pieces of pie were topped with generous scoops of vanilla ice cream, and Mrs. Barrie, Sasha and Kim were bagging and boxing the leftovers.

Over by the pool, the music now was louder and more lively. Dance tunes, Kim thought, tapping her foot. Her eyes were dazzled by the scene

123

before her — the sparkle of the lanterns reflected in the pool, the bright clothes, the laughter and smiles, the clink of cocktail glasses. Suddenly there was a noise like a firecracker, then another and another. They were popping off the corks of champagne.

Mrs. Barrie sighed and wiped her hands on her apron. Sasha and Kim had vainly declined aprons. Kim had been lucky; Sasha ruefully inspected a splotch of ice cream on the skirt of her dress.

"What do you says, girls?" Mrs. Barrie eyed the now cleared picnic tables. "I, for one, am just about beat, and I don't think we can do anything else around here." Her eyes sparkled as she put an arm around each girl and hugged them close. "You did a great job! I'm so proud of you both."

"I'm proud of you, Mom," Kim said, giving her a kiss. "You did all the hard stuff."

"Way to go, Earthly Delights!" Sasha cheered. "I think we can pack the car and head home — how about it?"

"I'm ready," said Kim, her eyes glued to where Chan stood at the bar surrounded by his friends, raising his glass as if to make a birthday speech. Well, she might as well go home. She *was* tired. And while Chan had been particularly warm to her before, he'd obviously forgotten about her now. Which was just as well — she'd never fit in with a crowd like this.

Before she could second the motion to go, Kim felt a strong arm on her shoulder. It was Chan. The stereo was playing a slow song now. "You missed the birthday toast, Kim, but you can't turn down the birthday boy's invitation to dance the first song with him."

Kim vaguely heard her mother saying, "Go on and stay, dear, have a good time. Sasha will give me a ride home in her car, and I'll leave the wagon for you." She felt herself gently propelled to the grassy area that had been cleared for dancing, and suddenly she was in Chan's arms, the glow of the Japanses lanterns like a spotlight on them, all his friends watching. One by one the other couples joined in, but for just a moment, Kim felt like she and Chan were the only two people in the world.

It might have sounded corny, but she knew what she was feeling was magic. There was no other word for it. She was dancing under the stars with Chan Lawrence, the tennis star, his broad shoulders and muscular arms wrapping around her and holding her close to his chest. It just couldn't be real.

I can't believe I had any doubts about him, Kim thought, any doubts that this attraction might not be right. Mom said to go with the flow and I did and look where it brought me! This *has* to be the real thing.

Chan was smiling down at her. "We're really hitting it off, huh Kim?" She nodded, smiling back at him. "A lot of girls out there are mighty jealous that I picked you out of the crowd for this special dance." He picked *me*, Kim was thinking. *Wow!*

"Kim, how would you like to be my date at the Newport International Tennis Tournament over the Fourth of July?"

It was so natural to be moving along with Chan, their bodies swaying slowly to the sensuous music, Kim couldn't have imagined contradicting him in any way. Besides, he didn't wait for an answer. He told her all the details of the trip.

"What better chance," he was saying, his lips so close to her ear that Kim could feel his warm breath on her neck, "for us to *really* get to know each other?" He kissed her neck and Kim felt her body catch fire. "Because we're only just starting now."

"Oh, Chan, it sounds wonderful," Kim said, "I'd love to go with you. If my parents think it's okay...."

"You just make sure they do." He looked deep into her eyes. "It would be so great for me to have you by my side, my number one fan."

At that moment, Kim didn't think there was anything she'd like better than to be Chan Lawrence's number one fan. And when he kissed her, she was positive.

As they neared the Barries' house, Sasha was glad the evening was almost over. She'd planned to stay over with Kim and had left an overnight bag at her house; hopefully she wouldn't stay too late at the Lawrences'. . . . Sasha sighed.

Mrs. Barrie glanced at her as Sasha pulled the car into the driveway. "I guess we're thinking the same thing, Sasha. But Kim's a big girl, she's old enough to make her own choices."

"I know, Mrs. Barrie." Sasha gathered an armful of leftovers and headed for the kitchen door. "I just can't help thinking that Chan isn't the person she thinks he is. And that Woody . . . oh, poor Woody!!"

Mr. Barrie was waiting for them in the kitchen, a fresh pot of coffee on the stove. He wanted to hear all about the party, but first he told Sasha that Woody had called to talk to both her and Kim.

While Mr. and Mrs. Barrie chatted, Sasha poured herself a tall glass of orange juice and considered calling Woody. She was sure he just wanted the scoop on the evening, and what could she say? The party was an unqualified success, and last I saw her, Kim was slow dancing off into the sunset with your favorite person, Chan Lawrence. Hardly. It would be telling enough that she was home and Kim wasn't. Better not to call at all — Woody would hear the news soon enough.

Sasha said good-night to the Barries. "I think I'll wait up for Kim in bed with a book."

"Thanks again so much for your help, honey." Mrs. Barrie pecked her cheek.

Sasha tried to read for a while; she had brought a copy of *A Tale of Two Cities* with her, and while that had seemed funny in light of her joking with her parents earlier, now it only seemed dismal.

She turned off the lights, but she was too keyed up to sleep; as soon as she got her mind off Kim and Woody and Chan, pictures of Rob Kendall and Wesley popped into her head instead. She tossed and turned for what seemed like hours. Finally she heard the sound of a car turning into the driveway.

Kim tiptoed into the bedroom, turning a light on low so not to wake Sasha. Just as she came abreast of Sasha's bed, Sasha sat up abruptly and hissed, "Boo!"

"So this is it," Sasha said in a low voice. "You're breaking up with Woody?" She hadn't meant for her words to sound cold, but they did. "Bjorn Borg really swept you off your feet, huh?" This last one was intended to lighten up the mood, but Sasha heard the underlying sharpness she just couldn't conceal.

Kim caught her breath. "Sasha, I thought you understood what I was going through."

"I do, Kim." Sasha twisted her hands in the blanket. She had to be honest with Kim about how she felt, even if it hurt her. "I just don't think you're going about what you're going through in the right way."

Kim stared at her. When she spoke, her voice was level, but icy. "Chan invited me to go to Newport, Rhode Island, for a big, important championship tournament."

Sasha was stunned. "When?"

"It starts on July third. We'd fly up tomorrow."

"Great, never mind the pet wash."

"In the *afternoon* tomorrow. After the pet wash."

"Kim, you just met this guy and you're ready to spend a weekend with him? Have you even talked to your parents about it?" Sasha was more concerned than shocked, but she knew she was coming across like a nag.

"Since when do I have to ask permission about

what I do?" Kim's eyes filled with tears. "You don't have any right to be so nasty about this."

"And you don't have any right to talk like that to someone who's just trying to be your friend." Sasha was out of bed and pulling on a pair of jeans. She didn't even bother to take off her nightgown; her T-shirt went on over it.

"I'm going home," she announced.

She stood hesitantly for a moment. She and Kim had never had a fight like this before; she hated the way it felt. But Kim was standing with her back to her; Sasha grabbed her things and ran downstairs.

She jumped into the VW Rabbit and drove home as fast as she could, which wasn't very fast because she could barely see the road through her tears.

Because her parents thought she was staying at Kim's, she had to wake them up to let her in; they'd bolted the door from the inside. Mr. Jenkins opend the door, his face sleepy and surprised. Once inside, she burst into tears. Her father gave her a long hug and then they sat on the stairs. Sasha spilled the whole story.

He put a comforting arm around her shoulders. "Growing up can be mighty rough," he said.

"I thought I was all grown-up," she answered in a small voice, "too grown-up to pick a fight with my best friend."

"You are, most of the time." Mr. Jenkins laughed ruefully. "Usually I feel grown-up, but not always. Maybe nobody ever really grows up, but we keep trying. You hang in there."

Chapter
12

Sasha rode into the parking lot of the animal shelter at nine o'clock the next morning. The ride over had been wonderful. It was a beautiful summer morning, the air was fresh and clear and warm, not too hot — just right. She'd turned down the offer of a ride from Wes just to get a chance to pump her legs. The exercise had invigorated her; her spirits were high.

Scarlett O'Hara was right, Sasha thought. Tomorrow *is* another day, and now it's tomorrow and I feel like a new person.

The smile on her face turned to an ear-to-ear grin when she caught sight of the pet washing committee. Ted was wearing thigh-high fisherman's waders; Phoebe had on a pair of old jeans that had been patched so many times there was hardly an inch of denim to be seen; Brenda was wearing a bright red T-shirt that said ALL WASHED UP; Peter and Monica wore matching yellow slickers and rain hats; Henry had sewn up mock pairs of surgical scrubs.

"Looks like I fit right in!" Sasha called out, laughing. She was wearing the very oldest shorts she could find and a tattered cotton shirt that her father claimed to have worn in college.

The chief washer, Woody Webster, was nowhere in sight, however, Sasha noted with a twinge of dismay. What if he was too mortified to face Kim and didn't come? But no, he must have been there earlier — someone had set up three old-fashioned laundry tubs and attached hoses to the building. Bottles of pet shampoo and brushes and combs marched in orderly rows.

Wes took over as leader in Woody's absence. "Check the water temperature — it should be warm. I don't think our canine customers would appreciate a cold shower!"

They already had a few customers, too, Sasha observed enthusiastically, and more cars were pulling into the lot even now. The pet wash was going to be a great success, she just knew it!

The gang was making a real show of hustling and bustling, but they didn't know where to start. Peter had hold of a hose, Chris was armed with a bottle of shampoo, Wes pushed back his sleeves with determination. You'd think they were going into battle! Sasha giggled. And battle against . . . a little boy with a beagle; a wrinkled-looking Chinese Sharpei belonging to a plump old man who more than slightly resembled his dog; a finely coiffed poodle led by a woman with dark curly hair.

Phoebe turned to Sasha, her eyes bright with mischief. "Do you see what I see?" she whispered. "It's true what they say about people choosing pets that look like them!"

"Okay," Wes said, "who wants to be the one to start things off?"

As if on cue, the oddest animal imaginable came bounding out of the shelter building. It had brown, shaggy hair, a long skinny tail, and legs that didn't match — the front pair was shorter than the back. One ear stood up rakishly.

It did a cartwheel, then a back flip with a splash in Sasha's tub. "Woof!" it barked in a voice that sounded like Woody's.

Sasha giggled.

"Woof, woof!" it barked insistently, dipping a pawful of water up and splashing it under its arm.

Sasha was doubled over with laughter. "Are you sure that coat of yours is washable?" she asked weakly.

"Arf," Woody answered. He grabbed a bottle of shampoo, but then thought better of it when Sasha pretended she really was going to give him a lather. He hopped out of the tub and hightailed it back to the shelter. The gang howled.

Now the pet wash really got going. Each tub had a team — one washer, one rinser, and the rest of the crew was on grooming duty. Chris had even brought a hair dryer and a bunch of extension cords.

"Any dog who's anybody is blow-drying its hair these days!" she said archly. When Woody reappeared, recognizable again in his red suspenders, she gave his wet head a few blasts.

Sasha kept looking over her shoulder for Kim. She was sure Kim had woken up this morning feeling sorry and silly about their falling out, too. It would feel so good to hug and make up.

Just then Kim did arrive — in Chan's black convertible Mercedes. At the same time, Rob Kendall strolled into the parking lot with a beautiful golden retriever — and the beautiful blond Cathy. And to top it all off, in pulled the WBBB van, and Laurie Bennington poured out of it.

To keep her eyes from Rob and Cathy — she didn't even want to look at Kim and Chan — Sasha focused on Laurie, who looked very sharp in a gray miniskirt and bright orange top. She guessed Laurie's wardrobe didn't exactly run to dog washing togs. It was a good outfit for ordering the camera crew around in, though, she thought good-naturedly.

The gang had decided on a mini-telethon, because of the time constraint. The TV station would take about five minutes of pet wash action and broadcast it periodically during the day; the Humane Society had extra volunteers coming in to handle the phone calls. Peter and Monica had also written a short advertisement that had been shown yesterday; it was certainly partially responsible for the big turn out.

Wes was staring at Kim and Chan, who had stopped by the van to talk to Laurie. "I can't believe Kim would ditch Woody, just like that," he said in a low voice to Sasha.

"It wasn't exactly just like that," Sasha said, squirting some shampoo into her hand. "I think she's just confused. She needs a breather from her relationship with Woody and this guy Chan just happened to come along at the right time."

Wes shook his head stubbornly. Sasha knew what he was thinking; with Wes everything was either black or white.

"It's wrong," he said, taking a dripping miniature schnauzer from Sasha and spraying it lightly with the hose.

"How can you say something like that is right or wrong?" Sasha asked. "People change — their feelings change."

"I'm only glad that can't happen to us," he said, pulling her to him, suds and all. "My feelings won't change."

Sasha returned his hug feebly. She felt his lips on her hair, but the usual tingle was lacking.

The camera crew was set up and ready to start shooting; as quick as a wink Laurie was asking Henry and Janie if she and Chan could usurp their tub for a few minutes.

"The two guest stars," Ted whispered into Sasha's ear. Sasha glanced quickly around for Woody, wondering how he was reacting to the arrival of Kim and Chan. She saw him towel drying and grooming a German shepherd puppy, his face a mask of concentration. Good for you, Woody, she thought, her heart aching with pride and affection. Don't let anyone see that you give a fig for Chan Lawrence.

The cameras were rolling; everyone was lathering and rinsing and combing and smiling for all they were worth. Rob and Cathy were next in line with their retriever; oh, please don't come to my tub, Sasha prayed.

The next thing she knew Wes was lifting the retriever into their tub.

"Sasha!" Rob greeted her with pleasure. "Hi, Wes. How's business?"

"Oh, it's great," Sasha said with false enthusiasm. She wiped her forehead with a damp hand. Cathy looked at her and smiled, and Sasha was sure she must have soap suds in her hair.

"I'm glad all your planning paid off," he continued. "This is Bonnie, by the way, the Petersons' dog."

"Well, Bonnie, let's get you beautiful." Sasha attempted to keep her face bright, partly because Wes was looking on suspiciously, partly because she didn't want her face flashed on cable television with a sourpuss expression.

She needn't have worried about the latter. The cameras were definitely focusing on Laurie and Chan, who certainly made a glamorous pair. There didn't seem to be any danger of an attraction there, though; each one was most concerned with looking his or her best.

Ted suddenly burst into hearty laughter. Sasha flashed him a "What's so funny?" look and he pointed. A dog that would make a Great Dane look like a puppy was standing in front of Chan and Laurie's tub.

"Laurie was probably hoping for a Chihuahua," someone joked.

Instead she found herself gingerly shampooing an Irish wolfhound. Chan stood aside, ready with the hose. He obviously didn't want his neatly pressed tennis whites dirtied. Woody's one concession to the tennis star's presence was a dry, "I'm surprised he didn't bring his racket," in Sasha's ear. He didn't even acknowledge Kim.

Laurie's outfit, meanwhile, wasn't going to be spared. The gigantic dog splashed her with muddy water and suds. She managed a smile, mostly because she was facing the camera. The dog leaned all its wet weight against her orange shirt. She patted it with what could have passed for good humor and affection.

Brenda scoffed. "Will you look at her?" she muttered under her breath. "Next thing you know, she'll be playing the lead in her own series!"

"It's not what you know, it's who you know," Brad agreed.

The telethon footage ended with Chan Lawrence, tennis star, speaking earnestly into the camera against a backdrop of laughing wet kids and barking dogs. Sasha couldn't help but notice that Kim looked kind of like a politician's wife, standing off slightly to the side and gazing at Chan with adoring eyes. Not the role Sasha would have expected a liberated young woman like Kim to play.

Sasha and Wes had finished with Bonnie; Phoebe brushed the golden retriever until she shone. Rob handed Sasha a ten-dollar bill.

"For the animal shelter," he said with a smile. "I think you guys did a fantastic job. See you around, Sasha."

Sasha watched Rob, Cathy, and Bonnie leave with a lump in her throat. Ted and Chris relieved her and Wes at tub number three, and the two took a breather, sitting down under a tree. In a minute, Sasha was to head for the office to help Helen; they expected the first broadcast of the pet wash to bring in not only pledge calls, but visitors hoping to adopt an animal.

Wes was holding her hand quietly, watching the pet wash hijinks with amusement. Sasha was watching Kim and Chan hop back into the Mercedes and pull briskly away from the curb. Through the cloud of exhaust, Sasha could read the license plate: CHAN 1. She chuckled. She supposed she had to give him credit; he was incredibly conceited, but at least he didn't try to hide it.

Wes gave her hand a warm squeeze. "Hey, what do you say we go pick out a puppy to adopt, you and me?"

"A puppy?" Sasha laughed. "What on earth do you want with a puppy?"

"It would be for you," Wes explained. "We could both train it, and then starting next summer when I'll be away for most of the time, it can keep you company. And by the time I'm a commissioned ensign in the Navy, on carrier duty or TDY — "

"TDY?"

"Temporary duty — away from base — maybe our puppy will have puppies! A lot of Navy wives have dogs even before they have children because their men are away so often."

"That'll really keep me busy," Sasha said lightly. She wished Wes wouldn't talk like this; it only emphasized in her own mind the gulf that was widening between them. Here he was, talking as if they'd always be together, someday get married, while she was thinking how little it seemed they had in common anymore. And how much she wished there wasn't any such girl as Cathy Silver.

Sasha sighed. Wes misinterpreted her silence and her sigh and turned to put his arms around her and pull her down on the grass. He kissed her slowly and she kissed him back. Yes, the fireworks still went off when she and Wes kissed, but maybe that wasn't enough anymore.

Before Sasha could pull away, she and Wes were doused with a bucket of cold water. They jumped to their feet laughing and sputtering. Woody stood there looking innocent. "Just putting out the fire," he said with a sly wink. "Now get back to work, you bums!"

Sasha was glad for the diversion. Walking back toward the group, Wes reminded her that they might want to cut out a little early, so she could go home and pack for the weekend at Sherwood Forest.

"And we'll pass the word to the whole gang before we leave that everybody's invited to my folks' cottage for a swim and cookout on the Fourth, then on to the Academy for the fireworks. How does that sound, sweetheart?"

"That sounds fine, Wes," Sasha said. But it didn't feel fine. Especially since that still left Saturday and Sunday night at Annapolis with Wes's parents. And they already knew that she was the girl he wanted to marry.

Chapter
13

"How did it go?" asked Mrs. Barrie, as Kim tore into the kitchen with only a few minutes to pack for her trip to Newport.

"What? Oh, the pet wash! Okay, I guess," she answered, opening the refrigerator and pulling out half a peach pie left over from the barbecue.

"Was Woody there, or am I not supposed to ask?" Mrs. Barrie, as usual, was interested, but she tried not to intrude.

Kim gave her a crooked smile as she dug into the pie without even bothering to cut a piece. "He was there. I heard he arrived decked out in a doggy suit! I was late — I missed his act." The smile stretched into a grin, in spite of itself. "You should have been there though, Mom. I did see him climb a tree to rescue a kitten. And the whole pet wash went over so well — you wouldn't have believed the crowd!"

What Kim didn't tell her mother was that Woody hadn't said a word to her the entire time, and that she couldn't blame him; she'd spent all of her brief stop at the fund-raiser glued to Chan Lawrence.

Kim grabbed a few more bites of pie and sprinted for the stairs, nearly decking her father, just coming in from a game of golf.

"You still here?" he said, mussing her hair affectionately, "I thought you'd be in Newport by now."

"Yeah, I'm running late, Dad." Kim tried to dodge around him, but he blocked her and grabbed both her arms, swinging her up into the air. "Let's just make sure we've got this straight, my girl. I know I'm an overprotective parent, but after all, you're only seventeen."

"Oh, Daddy," Kim smiled and rolled her eyes, wiggling to get free.

"I won't put you down until you tell me about the arrangements once more."

"Okay, you win. I'll be gone two nights. Mr. and Mrs. Lawrence will both be there to chaperone me. I have my own room at the hotel. How does that sound?"

"That sounds good." He put her down and spanked her lightly.

"We know we can trust you, honey," Mrs. Barrie called after Kim's rapidly retreating back. "And remember, if the fast track is too fast for you, just call us and we'll get you home."

Kim glanced around her room. She'd laid out the clothes she was taking; packing would only take a second. She looked at her watch: five whole minutes until Chan would be back to pick her up.

She reached for the phone and started to dial Sasha's number, then hung up. She wanted to apologize. She hadn't had a chance at the pet wash; they hadn't even made eye contact.

But now wasn't the time. She had to put Sasha and Woody and the whole gang behind her for the weekend. She had to be good company for Chan.

Kim threw her things into a small suitcase: black-and-yellow-checked pants, yellow shirt, white shorts, pink T-shirt, two brightly colored T-shirt dresses, one dressier dress, loose white jacket, underwear, shoes.

The doorbell rang just as she finished stuffing a few essentials into her shoulder bag. She ran to answer it, her heart galloping madly.

Chan stepped in and gave her a quick kiss. "All set, Tatum?" he asked.

"Tatum?" she repeated, puzzled.

"John McEnroe and Tatum O'Neal. You know, world famous tennis champion and beautiful young actress, currently a hot couple. Me McEnroe, you Tatum," he laughed. "Or to be more accurate, move over, McEnroe and Tatum, here come Lawrence and Kim."

Her parents joined them in the front hall and she hugged them both good-bye.

"Take care of yourself," Mr. Barrie said. Kim's mother just smiled her support. "And best of luck in the tournament, Chan!"

Chan grabbed Kim's suitcase and took her by the hand. They ran laughing to the car parked at the curb. Kim was surprised when a uniformed chauffeur emerged to hold the door for her. She tried to appear as if she rode in limousines every day.

"And away we go!" Chan joined her in the backseat, his bronzed handsome face glowing with high spirits. The smile he gave her was intoxicating.

Kim was thrilled to be in a limo with Chan racing to the airport, but one thing bothered her. His parents weren't there, unless they were riding in the trunk. She swallowed her question, not wanting to seem childish in front of the worldly, well-traveled tennis star. Besides, maybe Mr. and Mrs. Lawrence were meeting them at the airport.

And what's more, Kim reminded herself, I'm in control of my own life and I can take care of myself. I don't need Mr. and Mrs. Lawrence around to protect me from Chan.

Chan held Kim's hand as they settled into their first class seats on the shuttle to LaGuardia Airport in New York. She was ecstatic to be with Chan, but she wasn't so starry-eyed that she couldn't see that both Chan's parents and his coach were conspicuously absent. Finally, she couldn't contain herself any longer.

"Don't you usually travel with your coach to matches, Chan?" She tried to sound casual. "What about your parents?"

"Oh, Thompson." Chan's face darkened. "Sometimes I've just got to get that guy off my back. He really needs to learn who's on top. I'm the *player* and I'm the *winner* — he's not my boss!"

Kim was startled by Chan's sneering tone but before she had a chance to think about his words, he'd turned and touched her cheek, then kissed her lightly.

"I told Ned and my parents to go ahead — I'd wait and take a later flight so I could be with you. This is really something special, Kim, having you come with me to this match. I want you to know that!"

He emphasized his words with a long, deep look into her eyes. Kim was only too happy to believe him. He'd gone to extra trouble, maybe even gotten in a fight with his coach, all because he wanted her with him. That could only mean one thing, she thought, with a flush of excitement. Me and Chan Lawrence. *Wow!*

Sasha and Wes were watching TV at her house. Wes was eager to get going to Sherwood Forest; Sasha was not. She was stalling now by waiting for the next play of the pet wash broadcast; she wanted her parents to see it and it would be on any minute.

Wes restlessly checked his watch again. He stood up. Just then the cable program cut to the parking lot at the Rose Hill Humane Society. "That's us!" Sasha squealed. "Mom and Dad, come here! It's on!"

Mr. and Mrs. Jenkins hurried into the den. They laughed heartily at Laurie's discomfort as she wrestled with the sudsy Irish wolfhound and applauded Woody's rescue of the kitten. When the camera scanned Sasha and Wes at their tub all four cheered.

"But who's that with Kim?" Mrs. Jenkins asked. The screen was nearly filled by Chan's blond hair and blue eyes. "That's Chan Lawrence, isn't it?" She raised an eyebrow at her daughter.

Sasha sighed. "It's a long story — I'll tell you about it later, but in a nutshell it looks like Woody and Kim broke up."

"That's too bad," murmured Mr. Jenkins, stroking his soft brown beard. "They're such nice kids. On the other hand, I sometimes — often — think it's a great mistake to get too solidly locked into a relationship too early in life. Sometimes, all your friends get so accustomed to your being a couple that you never have a chance to find a more suitable life partner. Probably one of the reasons for the high divorce rate."

He was careful not to look at Wes, but Sasha knew he was talking about her. He and her mom had been part of the anti-war movement of the sixties and he was still very much opposed to what he called "the military mentality." The only reason he had accepted Wes as Sasha's boyfriend was because he liked and respected Wes as a person, even if he did not agree with his ideology. More important, he respected his daughter and trusted her judgment in forming friendships.

There was no question in Sasha's mind, however, that her father and mother hoped and expected that, while she and Wes might be a couple during high school and even into college, they'd break off their relationship eventually.

The telethon was over and Mrs. Jenkins ran to call in her pledge before she forgot.

"How about a quick meal?" she called in from the kitchen. "You two must be starving!"

"My parents are expecting us," Wes politely

declined. He looked pointedly at Sasha. Still dragging her feet, she went to her room for her suitcase. After one false start — she almost forgot the hostess gift she'd picked out so carefully — she was as ready as she'd ever be.

Sasha hugged her parents in the kitchen before she left, making one last effort to get out of the trip.

"Are you *sure* you don't need me in the bookstore?"

"Afraid not. Although we'd love to keep you here with us."

Mr. Jenkins put a hand on Wes's shoulder and smiled. "We figure it's only fair to share you every now and then. Drive carefully, Wes."

Wes talked enthusiastically all the way to Annapolis. Sasha had rarely seen him so animated, and for a moment her pulse quickened just like in the old days. She thought Wes was excited merely to be spending a weekend with her. But soon she realized by the frequency with which words like *academy* and *commander* came up in his conversation that it was the whole Navy thing that was thrilling him.

They'd passed through the city and now they were driving through real Maryland countryside. Sasha loved all the neat little farms, the miles of fences covered with honeysuckle. Too soon, they were bumping down a dirt road. The sign at the turnoff said CROW'S NEST.

Wes pulled the Corvette to a stop in front of a two-story house with a wide wraparound porch. Its shingles were weathered to a soft silvery shade.

Sasha jumped from the car, enchanted. The delicious smell of salt water erased all her worries about meeting Wes's parents. She could glimpse the bay, blue and sparkling, through the trees.

Wes watched her with proud eyes. Sasha met them and smiled. "It's a beautiful place," she said, sincerely.

He pulled their bags from the trunk and joined her. "Sasha, I'm so happy to introduce Sherwood Forest to you, and you to Sherwood Forest. Come on!"

The door was unlocked. They entered together.

"Anybody home?" Wes called out. He led Sasha into a big living room with a massive fieldstone fireplace. Sasha took a deep breath — she loved that vacation house smell.

Wes put the suitcases down and took Sasha's hand. He towed her through a door on the right, into a large kitchen, then onto a back porch that appeared to serve as the dining room. Still no parents. They walked back through the living room to peek into a large, and empty, study. It was a true summer cottage room, with nautical knickknacks in the bookshelves and on the walls, and two sets of bunk beds.

They heard a noise in the back of the house, and Wes pulled Sasha back to the porch. His parents were walking briskly up a steep path from the bay. It looked to Sasha like they'd been sailing. She felt her palms go damp with nervousness. Watching them approach, she was struck by how much Wes resembled his father. She realized it was their short haircuts and military bearing.

"Mother," Wes said, "may I present Sasha

Jenkins. Sasha, I'd like you to meet my mother, and my father."

Mrs. Lewis clasped Sasha's hand warmly. "It's so nice to finally meet you, dear," she said, in a low, sweet voice. She was a neat, small woman dressed in white trousers and a navy-and-white striped jersey. Her eyes were so sincerely welcoming that Sasha couldn't resist smiling broadly back.

Sasha turned to Wes's father. "And Mr. Lewis — I mean, Commander Lewis! I've heard so much about you as well." Oops, Sasha thought, smothering a grin.

"Welcome aboard," Commander Lewis said with a wink.

They were a very nice couple, Sasha had to admit. There was no denying they were going out of their way to make her feel at ease, and out of natural good feeling — nothing forced here.

Sasha remembered her gift, and ran to get the package from her bag. She gave it to Mrs. Lewis with a shy smile. It was a book, but Sasha had no idea whether it was one that would appeal to Wes's mother. She'd just taken a chance — it was published by the Naval Institute Press and had been on the best-seller list for ages. It was out in paperback now, but she'd brought the hard-cover, because it was so much nicer.

"Aren't you sweet?" said Mrs. Lewis. "May I unwrap it now?"

Sasha nodded, holding her breath. Mrs. Lewis carefully removed the bow and gift paper then held up the fat volume for everyone to see.

"How wonderful! *The Hunt for Red October*,"

she said. Her green eyes, so like Wes's, smiled at Sasha. "I've been dying to read it. Thank you so much, dear."

Commander Lewis lifted the book gently but firmly from her hand. "I'll fight you for it," he laughed heartily. "I'll read it first. Then I'll tell you all about it."

"Not on your life," she said, snatching it back with a smile.

The commander looked over at Sasha and grinned. At that moment, he looked like an older version of Wes — the same chiseled features and casual, but erect posture. Only his short hair was graying. He stabbed a thumb in his wife's direction. "She thinks she's an admiral. I don't want to disillusion her, so I've never told her otherwise."

The men laughed and Mrs. Lewis shook her head scoldingly. She took Sasha's arm. "I'll show you your room, dear."

The two of them went up the stairs to the second floor. "Here's where you'll stay, Sasha, and the head is right next door."

"The head?"

"Oh, I'm sorry. The bathroom, dear. That's habit, using Navy talk. You'll get the hang of it. It doesn't take long. It's easier than learning French and a lot more fun."

Sasha was charmed by her room. It was tiny, but perfect. The walls were warmly paneled and hung with the obligatory pictures of sailboats; the twin beds were covered with cheerful white counterpane bedspreads.

Mrs. Lawrence excused herself. "I have to get

back downstairs to supervise the buffet supper. You take some time to settle in, Sasha."

When Wes's mother left, Sasha opened the bedroom window and slowly inhaled the salty air. The weather was perfect — balmy and clear, with a teasing summer breeze that seemed to promise a romantic summer night. Wes would be coming by later to steal away with her for a long walk on the beach this evening, and had even plucked a soft pink flower for Sasha to wear in her hair. Hearing the waves made Sasha wish she could fit into the life at Sherwood Forest. But the more she learned about Wes and his background, the more she knew she would never fit in.

Chapter
14

The shuttle to LaGuardia hit turbulence. The plane bounced constantly; the seat belt sign was on for the entire flight. Kim was thankful she had a strong stomach — she would have died of embarassment if she'd been sick.

The pilot had to circle the field, then come in quickly through a momentary break in the cloud cover to land. Rain slanted across the tarmac as hand in hand, Chan and Kim ran for the charter helicopter that would take them and four other passengers on to Newport.

Chan's usually sunny disposition had turned as foul as the weather. Kim was shocked by some of the words that burst through his clenched teeth. He apologized when he noticed her alarmed expression, but his mood didn't lighten.

"Darned weather," he snorted. "Darned dog wash. I knew we should have left last night. This morning at the very latest. If I'm not there by six to register for my first match tomorrow, I'll default."

Kim was a little put off by the implication that it was her fault, but she understood how disappointed Chan would feel if he missed the match.

Chan leaned forward to speak to the pilot. "Let's get going," Chan said, his voice hard and aggressive. "*Now*."

Kim's eyes widened at his rudeness, but the pilot was unruffled.

"I'm going to wait a few minutes longer to make my decision," he said evenly. "The rain is really coming down hard."

Before Chan could press the pilot further the clouds broke. They took off, and in an instant the mood in the helicopter switched from gloom and anger to giddiness. Chan kidded and laughed and told stories about people and incidents Kim had never heard of. She laughed anyway, she was so relieved by the change in atmosphere. She was glad that Chan Lawrence was back to the person she recognized.

When they disembarked in Newport, Chan ushered Kim into his waiting limo. Kim was more than a little nervous by the time they reached the hotel. She was happy to see Chan's parents waiting for them in the lobby. Kim was already registered, in her own room.

"It wasn't easy to pull it off," Mr. Lawrence told her, giving her a big wink. "Town's crowded but we pulled a few strings. Can't have Chan's girl sleeping in the hallway."

Kim followed a bellhop into the elevator leaving Chan to take care of his registration for the

151

tournament. The bellhop unlocked a spacious room and put her suitcase on the luggage stand.

He opened the draperies and waited. Kim stared at him blankly. What was she supposed to do now, ask him to stay for a drink? Oh, the tip! She handed him a dollar and he thanked her and left. As soon as the door closed behind him, she burst out laughing.

She bounced on one of the double beds and surveyed the room. Desk, double dresser, easy chair, coffee table, TV, and a carpet so thick you could sink in it up to your knees.

She jumped up and looked into the bathroom. It was so elegantly equipped she just had to try it out. She peeled off her clothes and popped into the shower. The water pulsed like a massage. There was a steam setting, too, so she had a steam bath. Then she pushed a button and miraculously, the steam disappeared.

She washed her hair and used the built-in blow-dryer. "All this place needs is a Jacuzzi," she said out loud. And lo and behold, the deep bathtub had jets built in all the way around the rim.

So this was how the other half lived! Kim was impressed. Although, she rationalized, the Jacuzzi was simply practical in a hotel catering to sports-men and women. Tennis players and America's Cup sailors worked their bodies to the limit. Lying in a Jacuzzi would be great therapy.

She planned to try it later. She could use some therapy herself after that nerve-wracking trip. Kim suddenly wished Sasha was there, so they could share the fun, so she'd have somebody to talk to besides herself.

There was a knock on the door. She opened it before she remembered she still had on her terry robe.

Chan whistled. Kim flushed and started to close the door, but he put a hand out and held it. "You knew I was coming, huh?" he teased. "Aren't you going to invite me in?"

Kim forced herself to smile, she hoped not *too* invitingly. "Sure, come in. I was just going to dress for dinner." Chan thought she was grown-up, that was why he'd invited her along on this trip. She didn't want to give away that she felt every bit as young as she was.

"You going to be comfortable here?" he asked, strolling casually around the room.

"Yes, very," she answered eagerly. "This is a fantastic room."

Chan sat down on one of the beds and looked at Kim. She swallowed and pulled her robe a little tighter around her waist. He certainly looked strikingly handsome, in white trousers and a navy blazer. "Come here, Kim, he said."

She approached him hesitantly. He pulled her so that she was sitting on his lap. Her heart pounded, but not from excitement, like it had the other times Chan had held her close. Kim felt her body stiffen. She smiled nervously.

"Dinner's not for half an hour," Chan said, in a low voice. He began to kiss her, on the mouth and then on the neck. Kim pushed him away. She jumped to her feet and retreated to the window, as far from the bed as possible.

"What's the matter with you?" Chan said irritably. Then he stood up and walked toward her. He put his hands lightly but firmly on her shoulders. "I just want to be with you, Kim. Don't you want to be with me, isn't that why you came?"

His tone was gentle again, and Kim relaxed just slightly. "Of course, Chan. But I have to get dressed now. I don't want to keep your parents and Mr. Thompson waiting."

Chan crossed his arms. "Don't let me stop you."

Kim blushed again. Her mind raced chaotically. Should I lock myself in the bathroom? Press the bell for the maid? Hit him with the Bible from the nightstand? She took a deep breath to calm herself. "I'd like some privacy, Chan. Can you come back for me in a few minutes?"

He shifted impatiently and Kim, afraid of offending him, softened her words with a hand on his arm. "Okay?" She reached up and kissed him lightly then stepped back with what she hoped looked like determination.

Chan shrugged, then threw his hands up with a laugh. "I'll never figure out women." He headed for the door, turning to look back at her before he left. "I like you just like that," he said, eyeing her robe, "but dinner in Newport is a formal occasion. See you in ten minutes, Kim."

Dinner in Newport *was* a formal occasion, Kim thought. She was glad she was a caterer, otherwise she wouldn't have recognized half the things on the elegant menu. She was also glad her mother had made her pack her one party dress, an aqua-and-white-flowered silk dress with a wide sash worn low at the waist.

The meal was fun because there wasn't a quiet

154

moment. She and the Lawrences and Ned Thompson, Chan's coach, had a central table and they might as well have been on stage. Everybody knew Chan. People stopped by to chat and joke and check out Chan's date. The general concensus seemed to be that she passed muster; everyone was friendly and admiring.

Kim's spirits were high again; seeing Chan in his element, the embodiment of cheer and assurance and physical grace, affected her like it had the first day she met him. She couldn't take her eyes off of him, and the charge she felt when his foot touched her under the table or his blue eyes held hers for a secret lingering moment made it almost impossible for her to concentrate on the conversation. Chan glowed from the attention; Kim knew she was glowing, too.

The only awkward element of the meal was Chan's coach, who was seated on Kim's other side. It was very apparent to Kim that he didn't approve of her being there. He ignored all her efforts at pleasant small talk.

After dinner, Chan walked Kim back to her room. She'd stopped floating; her feet were firmly on the ground and she was ready for Chan's move when it came.

Before she'd unlocked the door, he kissed her, long and hard. The kiss said: Make up to me for turning me out before. Chan only said, in a low, thrilling voice, "Aren't you going to be lonely in that big room all by yourself?"

"Not at all," Kim replied matter-of-factly. She grinned at Chan's surprised expression. "Goodnight, Chan!" She was in her room — alone —

with the door closed and locked before he could protest.

Kim flopped onto the bed and kicked off her high-heeled sandals. She rubbed her feet. She only wore them about once a year and that was too often.

She flung her arms out to the side and let out a deep sigh. She was exhausted. Lucky she didn't have to play tennis tomorrow!

Suddenly Kim felt lonely, but not for Chan. She realized she hadn't quite been prepared for his aggressive sophistication in the matter of romance. No, she was lonely for a friend, someone she could feel comfortable with, talk to openly.

Woody's face flashed into her mind — sweet, kind, adorable Woody. Kim sighed. She was so far from home. But even if she were in Rose Hill, there'd still be an unbearable distance between her and Woody. She had hurt him so badly, they could never be friends like that again.

Kim put on her nightgown and crawled between the cold, white sheets. She had a lot to think about this weekend.

The stands weren't full, apparently because today's matches were preliminaries. "Just wait until Chan is playing in the finals, center court!" Mr. Lawrence was saying.

Mr. Lawrence nudged Kim. Chan appeared on the court clad in white shorts and a red-and-white striped shirt. Even from the stands he looked dazzling. His opponent was wearing all white.

A voice boomed out over the P.A. system. Kim

jumped in her seat. "Mr. Lawrence and Mr. Ferris. Mr. Lawrence has won the spin for serve."

Chan and his opponent took their positions facing one another without exchanging a word. Neither was smiling. So much for tennis being fun, Kim thought.

Chan stood with his left side to the net, his weight on his right foot. In one fluid motion he rocked back, dropped both hands, shifted his weight to his left foot, and tossed the ball high. He cranked up the most wicked serve Kim had ever seen.

He aced it.

Mr. Lawrence shouted at the top of his lungs and pounded Kim on the shoulder. "That's my boy!"

The scorekeeper announced, "Fifteen-love."

Chan's next serve was called out.

"Are you blind?" yelled Mr. Lawrence furiously.

Kim sunk down in her seat. People sitting nearby were staring and sshh-ing. She didn't mind so much for herself — but if Chan could hear he must be very embarrassed.

Kim clapped politely whenever Chan had a winning shot — there were quite a few of them. She even managed to tune out Mr. Lawrence's loud cheering for Chan and heckling of the linemen. But she couldn't tune out her growing discomfort with her role as Chan's number one fan.

He was winning easily; Ferris just wasn't quite in his league. But that didn't stop him from contesting points and stalling for time. Not outrageous behavior certainly, but still. . . . The match seemed to Kim to last forever.

Finally Chan was shaking hands with his opponent. He had won in straight sets. The spectators applauded enthusiastically. Chan walked over to his bench to grab a towel and drape it around his neck. He took a shot of water from the bottle and waved to the crowd.

Mr. Lawrence dragged Kim down from the stands onto the court. She felt more than a little silly. Chan's father pounded him on the shoulder. "Way to go!"

"Congratulations!" Kim said.

Chan pulled her into a sweaty bear hug and gave her a very public kiss, just as a news camera focused on him.

"Nice game," said a reporter. "Would you introduce us to your girl?"

His arm around her shoulders, Chan turned to Kim to the camera. "Her name is Kim. Kim Barrie."

Kim smiled artificially.

"See you on the late news," the reporter said to Chan. "That is, if you win the next match this afternoon, right?"

Coach Thompson, who'd just about been invisible throughout the match, now whisked Chan away.

Mr. Lawrence followed, calling back to Kim something about showers, steam baths, rubdowns, naps, food.

Kim was happy to see Chan's father go. Now she could enjoy some tennis in peace.

Kim's stomach rumbled. She giggled. It

sounded just like Mr. Lawrence grumbling a bad call. Time for lunch, she decided. She walked back to the hotel's coffee shop.

She was surprised to see Mrs. Lawrence there, sitting at a table, all alone.

"Hi, Mrs. Lawrence. May I join you?" Kim asked with a bright smile.

Mrs. Lawrence looked up from the coffee she was absently stirring. For a second she seemed to have trouble focusing. Then her face cleared and she smiled.

"Oh, Kim. Yes, do. I'd love to have some company."

Kim ordered a hamburger and a double-chocolate milk shake. She glanced covertly at Chan's mother. Mrs. Lawrence seemed quieter and more distracted than usual, although as always she was very warm and sweet to Kim.

"You must be very proud of Chan," Kim said. She thought Mrs. Lawrence might want to hear about the match.

"You must be wondering why I wasn't there," said Mrs. Lawrence.

"Oh, I understand," Kim assured her. "All that anxious competition, it's not for everybody."

"It does make me uncomfortable." Mrs. Lawrence's face lit up at Kim's sympathy. "You see, dear, my husband has been in charge of Chan's career ever since he was a small boy."

Kim nodded, taking a bite of her hamburger.

"Chan's tennis is something *they* share — I've never much understood it, or felt a part of it. It's really a language they speak, and a culture, too, that's just foreign to me."

Kim had a sudden insight into her lonely life. Mrs. Lawrence had probably been pushed to the background years ago. Tennis was a father and son thing, with Mr. Lawrence picking out the first racket, the coaches, building the tennis courts at Wildcliff, pushing his son's budding career.

"I enjoyed watching Chan play, Mrs. Lawrence," said Kim, choosing her words carefully. "I know you must be happy about his win."

Chan's mother reached over and patted her hand. "You're good for Chan, dear. I'm so glad you two met. So glad you came." Her eyes misted. "It means so much to me to see Chan with a nice girl his own age, someone with an ordinary life that has nothing to do with tennis. How nice it would be if this tennis could be less of an obsession."

Kim squeezed Mrs. Lawrence's hand.

She brightened. "I do hope I'll see you often dear. Did you know that Chan, and his father of course, are going to Australia shortly?"

Kim shook her head.

Mrs. Lawrence studied her. "I do hope you'll go to Australia with Chan, dear. If you do, perhaps I shall go as well."

It sounded as if she wanted an ally; Kim knew just how she felt. "Why don't you go with me to the match this afternoon?" she asked impulsively.

Mrs. Lawrence hesitated. Kim was almost sure she'd say yes, until the older woman slowly shook her head. "Go," she said, warmly. "And think good thoughts for Chan."

Chapter
15

"Organization is the operative word, and everybody has a working part," Mrs. Lewis said to Sasha. With the help of a cook hired for the weekend, Wesley's mother was masterminding the evening's dinner party. She gave orders with the ease of years of practice.

"Sasha, you can set the table," she said. "You know where the cutlery is. Places for eight plus one, the white linen tablecloth and napkins, and fold the napkins nicely, dear."

"Who's the ninth guest?" Sasha asked curiously.

"That's just for In Case."

"Who is in case?"

"In Case somebody drops in. Then I can say, 'Join us, please. Your place is already there.' That way, In Case won't feel he's imposing."

Sasha laughed, her brown eyes sparkling. "That's funny, Mrs. Lewis. I like it here more and more." Her cheeks pinkened.

Kim Barrie popped into Sasha's mind. Kim would really open eyes around here. She was a fantastic cook, she knew all about setting elegant party tables. . . .

Kim.

Sasha missed her. There were more than just miles separating them. Sasha hoped Kim was having a good time, too, because she'd had time to think things over.

And Kim was right. She'd fallen out of love with Woody and in love with Chan. She'd had the courage of her convictions and she'd acknowledged her new love to herself.

And that's more than I can say, Sasha thought, suddenly sad. The picture of Rob — of Rob and her — kept finding its way into her mind. She closed a door on the image, one more time.

She sighed. In her case, there wasn't a reason anymore to leave Wes. Rob had somebody else. But the reason didn't have to be a person, she realized with a tight feeling in her heart. Her own feelings were a reason, and they had changed. Maybe it was time to be honest with herself — and with Wes.

Mrs. Lewis brought her back to earth. "Sasha, would you get the salad, please? It's in the refrigerator. Toss it and bring it with the vinegar and oil cruets. This is going to be a lovely supper."

After dinner, Sasha once again found herself alone with Wes's mother. Mrs. Lewis had spirited her away from the kitchen, where she'd been helping with the "K.P."

They sat on a couch in the study, smiling at

each other. She gave herself a quick mental pep talk: Okay, Sasha, this is it. Now's your chance to start opening up.

"Mrs. Lewis, it's so nice to finally meet you and Commander Lewis. But I'm afraid I'm not really ready to be treated as part of your world."

She held her breath, hoping Mrs. Lewis wouldn't take offense. Far from it, Wes's mother was only too happy for Sasha to confide her doubts to her.

"Dear, you're never too young to start," she said, giving Sasha's hand a friendly squeeze.

Wes broke up the chat. He stuck his head around the door of the study and smiled at the picture his mother and his girl friend made.

"Mom, can I steal Sasha away from you? It's a beautiful night, there's a little bit of a moon — perfect for a sail."

Mrs. Lewis took Sasha's hand and put it in Wes's. "She's all yours, dear."

Wes smiled knowingly at Sasha. She felt her heart racing as they made their way hand in hand down the path to the shore. It was a perfect night for summer romance. She could feel what Wes was thinking by the warmth that shot from his palm straight up her arm: They were finally alone. She wanted to be alone, too, but for different reasons.

Wes was an excellent sailor; he quickly had the small boat under sail. The cool evening air felt good on Sasha's flushed cheeks. She was glad for the light breeze that whipped her long hair across her face, hiding her anxious expression.

Wes wasn't distressed when shortly the wind

died down and they found themselves becalmed. He let go of the tiller and pulled Sasha next to him.

"All the easier to put my arms around you," he said softly, nuzzling her hair. "You passed her entrance exam, Sasha," Wes was saying, his lips on her neck, close to her ear. "Everybody loves you."

Sasha pushed him away. "Wes, stop." Her voice cracked. Tears filled her eyes, blurring the vision of the confusion on Wes's face. "It's not working. I . . . I can't."

"What's the matter? What's wrong? Did something upset you?" His voice shook with concern as he pulled her close again.

Sasha caught her breath, stifling a sob. "No, don't Wes — don't touch me. Please."

His arms fell to his sides, his eyes, intensely green even under the dim light of the young moon, shone with hurt. "What have I done, Sasha? What am I doing wrong? Why can't I touch you?"

"I can't think when you touch me — I just can't think. And I need to, to tell you . . . Wes, I just can't do it. I just can't be a Navy wife, now or ever." Sasha put her fists to her eyes and pressed as if she could keep the tears from flowing.

"I know it's a lot to think about, all that's ahead for me — and you. But we have plenty of time, Sasha. You don't need to feel like anybody's hurrying you — I would never want you to think that." He put his arm tentatively around her. When she didn't pull away, he gripped her shoulders firmly.

Sasha shook her head. "But we don't have time, Wes. The Navy's like a — like a conveyor belt. Once you get anywhere near it it grabs you and just keeps moving you along."

"You've let my mom scare you with stories of Navy life, Sasha." He touched her hair gently. "It's not all as bad as it sounds. Don't you think they're happy? Don't you think they like their lives?"

Wes was surprised by the intensity in Sasha's wide brown eyes, still bright with tears. "Maybe they are, Wes, but I couldn't be. Not ever. Don't you see, all this time we've been together, I've been separating you from your beliefs, your values. I couldn't love the Navy but I loved you and that was all that mattered. And now, it's getting harder to do that, to find a Wes who isn't the Navy, too, and soon, next year at Annapolis, it'll be impossible."

Sasha swallowed, her throat aching.

Suddenly, Wes pulled back. "What are you saying, Sasha?" The tremor of emotion in his voice almost broke Sasha's heart.

"I'm saying I don't know — I just don't know if I love you anymore." Sasha's words fell upon the silence like stones into the water, sinking, sinking, gone forever. Sasha leaned over the side of the boat and trailed her hand in the water as if she could retrieve them, unsay them.

Wes spoke with a great effort. "Sasha, I understand. You're having doubts, that's natural. We can work things out; we *will* work them out. We have to — I love you."

Before Sasha could answer, the sound of an

outboard motor bounced across the water toward them.

"Need a tow?" Commander Lewis called out. The motorboat's lights flashed over them. In a few seconds, Wes's father had pulled up beside the sailboat and was cheerfully roping the two boats together.

Sasha was glad the dark night hid the fact that she'd been crying from Commander Lewis, and he was unaware of the tension in the atmosphere. My mom would feel it, Sasha thought, biting her lip to make her eyes stop smarting. And that's part of the problem; Wes is too much like his father and I'm too much like my mother.

Back inside the cottage, Wes and Sasha didn't have another chance to be alone.

Wes walked Sasha to the foot of the stairs after she'd wished everyone good-night, saying she was tired and wanted to get to bed early. He kissed her tenderly. "Good-night, Sasha. Sleep well. I love you."

She smiled weakly. She was too tired to talk anymore anyway. Maybe it was just as well. "Night, Wes," she said.

Chapter
16

Sunday flew by in a whirl of activity for Sasha. Between sailing, formal meals, and meeting more Naval officers and their wives at a picnic lunch that was held on the bay, she and Wes didn't have a minute of privacy. He sent her countless looks of love and understanding, but Sasha knew she couldn't show a love that was no longer there. It was an S.O.S. she just couldn't answer.

By Monday the Fourth — had it only been two days? — Sasha's face ached from smiling, her neck from nodding, her heart from being sweet and agreeable when she felt just the opposite. The only thing that kept her going was knowing her friends would all arrive at any minute for a Fourth of July cook-out.

When their caravan of cars pulled up in front of the cottage, she rushed out to fling her arms around each one of them in turn: Woody, Chris,

Ted, Phoebe, Brenda, and Brad.

These were the friends she saw every day of the week during the school year. Her very best friends; only Kim was missing. Sasha had never felt such an overwhelming surge of affection for them. Their smiles, their jokes and stories, those were things she could understand and be comfortable with.

"I'm so happy to see you!" Sasha said, nearly tackling Woody. "It feels like ages!"

"Haven't they been feeding you?" Woody asked, pretending to be concerned. "You look like a hungry animal at the zoo that's just escaped its cage."

Close, Sasha thought, very close, Woody. Out loud she said, "No, I'm just so happy to see you. Happy Fourth of July!"

Chris took her aside as Wes led the gang into the house for introductions. "Sasha, is something the matter between you and Wes? When you came out to meet us I could swear your eyes were saying 'Save me! Save me!' "

Sasha hugged her quickly. "They were. There is. And you are — saving me, I mean. Just by being here. I can't go into it right now . . . maybe tonight . . . back in Rose Hill."

Wes came back outside to round up the stragglers. "Come on," he said with a heartiness that Sasha knew was forced. "Everyone into their suits for a swim!"

They all raced down the path to the dock. Woody was first in, courtesy of the biggest belly flop ever.

Sasha swam out to join him. Woody's familiar

168

clowning made Sasha feel that if all wasn't quite right in the world it could be, and would be again.

"Race you back, Sasha!"

"You're on, Webster!"

A full-scale Fourth of July barbecue was under way when the gang trooped back up to the house to dry off and change. Sasha piled up a plateful of potato salad and fruit, strictly avoiding the hamburgers and ribs, and sat cross-legged on the lawn.

The Navy men were interested in Ted. They asked him if as a football player he had ever thought of trying for the Academy. Ted looked at Sasha as if to say, are we going to go through all *this* again?

He sidestepped the question neatly. "My fame on the football field is going to be nothing compared to Sasha — *she's* going to be a best-selling author."

Gee thanks, Ted! Sasha mouthed at him.

It was getting late in the afternoon.

"Time to go over to the Academy for the fireworks," Wes's father announced.

There was a sudden rush of activity. The Navy wives gathered up the remnants of the feast and headed for the kitchen. The Commander hath spoken, Sasha thought wryly.

Sasha had packed her bag and now she tossed it into Woody's car when Wes wasn't looking. She knew that was chicken; Wes thought she was staying another night. But all Sasha wanted to do now was go home, to Rose Hill and her parents. Things had to be resolved between her and Wes, but it could happen there just as easily as in Sherwood Forest. It was dark by the time they reached Annapolis.

Cars parked, they hiked the crazy, uneven brick sidewalks until they reached King George Street and the gates to the Academy. Their route took them past the imposing Field House and Farragut Field to the sea wall, where a crowd had already gathered.

They spread their blankets and made themselves comfortable. Chris and Ted sat with their arms around each other; Brenda and Brad snuggled. When Wes quietly took her hand, Sasha didn't pull away.

The first rockets burst and showered down in veils of green and gold into the Severn River. Sasha gasped with delight. Each display was more breathtaking than the last.

Wes turned to Sasha. "Are you having fun, Sasha?"

"The fireworks are wonderful," she answered. She tipped her head back to look up at the midnight velvet sky, which just then burst into green, blue, and white flowers. She couldn't bear to meet Wes's eyes. "They make me feel like a little girl, a kid again. They're so magical."

"Look at me, Sasha." Wes's voice was quiet, pleading. "Are you still mad at me?"

"Mad at you? Wes, I was never mad at you. Mad at us maybe, mad at myself mostly." A loud boom made them all jump. Chris shrieked.

"I just think we need to talk some more, Wes," she continued quietly. "If not tonight, tomorrow night. Sometime soon."

Wes gripped her hand. "Sasha, I know you and

I are different in a lot of ways but that doesn't matter to me. It really doesn't."

"Later," she whispered, putting a finger to his lips. "We'll talk later."

The grand finale of the show was upon them. A huge rocket burst high over their heads — it was a gigantic American flag made of a million fluttering red, white, and blue stars. Phoebe clapped wildly. Woody whistled. The whole crowd roared.

The spectators were dispersing, and the Lewises were packing the blankets and coolers now empty of soda into the cars that would be heading back to Sherwood Forest. Her own friends were discussing alternate routes home for avoiding traffic.

This was it. Sasha put a hand on Wes's arm. "Wes, I packed my things before we left this evening. My stuff's in Woody's car. I know you'd planned on my staying until tomorrow, but I — I want to go home."

Wes had stiffened. Now he turned to her with a grim face. "Sasha, I just don't understand you. You said you wanted to talk, and now you're running away from me!"

"But Wes, don't you see, we can't talk in Sherwood Forest." Her voice was sharp. "We're never alone: It's always Navy, Navy, Navy." Sasha closed her eyes briefly. "Wes, I'm sorry. I didn't mean to snap at you. I think we'll both be better off for a night apart to think things over."

His expression softened. He leaned toward her as if he expected to be pushed away, and when he wasn't he kissed her gently on the mouth.

"Just don't think too hard," he said, "and everything will be fine. I'll call you tomorrow night and we'll have dinner in Rose Hill, okay?"

"Okay, Wes."

Sasha said her good-byes to Commander and Mrs. Lewis, explaining that her parents needed her at the bookstore in the morning. They were gracious and affectionate; she almost felt guilty that she felt so relieved to be getting away.

"Good-night, Sasha," Wes said, kissing her one more time before turning to head for his own car. "Don't you forget — you're my O.A.O."

Sasha had never been so happy to be riding in Woody's Volvo.

Newport was burning with tennis fever and almost against her will, Kim caught it. Chan made it to the finals on the Fourth of July.

The semifinal match that morning had been a doozy. In terms both of the level of play and Mr. Lawrence's level of noise and rudeness, it made the first match Kim had watched look like a game of checkers.

Mr. Lawrence had pounded his fist on her shoulder so many times she was sure it would be black and blue for weeks. He'd stamped his feet and yelled. Finally, in self-defense, Kim relaxed and let her adrenaline flow. It *was* great tennis after all! She leaped out of her seat and screamed along with the audience the next time Chan won an exciting point. She turned and pounded Mr. Lawrence on *his* shoulder.

Kim was no longer on cloud nine where Chan

Lawrence was concerned. She wasn't even on cloud eight. Her feet were back firmly on the ground, and although half of her wanted to go home more than anything — she remembered her parents' promise of rescue with a pang — the other half insisted that she stick things out. You got yourself into this; now handle it like an adult.

Sunday night had witnessed another wrestling match with Chan at the door of her hotel room. Kim had again successfully evaded him. He clearly didn't like the idea that his efforts might fail; he called her room and tried to sweet-talk her over the phone.

They'd continued to enjoy each other's company — no one could deny that Chan Lawrence was handsome and charming; the most glamorous escort any girl could ask for. But the fireworks that his kisses set off inside her were just that, a brief and brilliant flash, with no real substance.

The semifinal match had cemented things in Kim's mind. The most charitable person on earth couldn't have described Chan's behavior on the court as anything but temperamental. And Mr. Lawrence's behavior in the stands was Chan's multiplied to the nth degree.

Mr. Lawrence had jumped up and down, shouting. When the official called for quiet he obeyed for all of three seconds, then shouted again. Silence was again requested.

Someone was taking flash pictures. This time it was Chan who stormed. He strutted over to the umpire and demanded a stop be put to the photography. He waved his racket for emphasis.

The match had been close and the tension high. Kim thought Mr. Lawrence might explode as he shouted, "Kill him, Chan!" — his face as red as a beet.

But Chan won before Mr. Lawrence had a coronary and now there were only the finals to survive. Kim left the court where Chan, Mr. Lawrence, and Coach Thompson were talking to reporters, no doubt discussing the inevitability of Chan's victory in the finals. She was ready for lunch, and she had a feeling she wouldn't have to eat alone.

She was right. She found Mrs. Lawrence in the coffee shop again. This time Kim sat down without waiting for an invitation.

"Would you come with me this afternoon?" she asked earnestly. "Please?"

Since the day before at lunch, Mrs. Lawrence and Kim had talked a number of times and Kim felt the new friendship was rewarding on both sides. Mrs. Lawrence was lonely on the fringes of her son's career; Kim was disappointed in her romance with Chan. But she hadn't been able to persuade her to come to a match.

The older woman traced a circle on the table with her forefinger. When she spoke, it was so low that Kim could hardly hear her. "I can't. I simply can't."

"But why, Mrs. Lawrence? He's your son. Shouldn't you be rooting for him, just this once in the finals, even if you don't like tennis all that much?"

Mrs. Lawrence raised her faded blue eyes to

look straight at Kim. "Perhaps I should, dear, but I want him to lose. Now you know."

Kim was shocked to the depths of her soul.

"Try to understand," Mrs. Lawrence went on. "I'm his mother. I never approved of this, never. I wanted more for Chan. I wanted him to lead a normal life, go to college, have a profession. I don't like what this is doing to him. *Or* to my husband."

"Then why did you come along?" Kim whispered. She placed her strong, brown hand on Mrs. Lawrence's frail, white one.

"To be here, if he loses. To try to find the words to convince him that it's all for the best. I don't suppose anything I could say would get through to either one of them, but I have to try."

Kim's heart ached with compassion. When she saw the glint of a tear in Mrs. Lawrence's eye, she gripped her hand tightly and smiled encouragingly.

"No, Mrs. Lawrence," she said, "you're wrong. I think they *would* listen to you if you would only tell them how you feel! You think they won't give you a chance to hear what you think about Chan's career."

Mrs. Lawrence smiled sadly at Kim. She wiped her eye with a scallop-edged handkerchief. "*You* know Chan, Kim dear, and you've seen my husband at the courtside. Chan has a mind of his own — he won't let anyone tell him what to do. His poor coach. . . . And my husband, he cares about winning even more than Chan does, I sometimes think. All that shouting — I often believe he's lost sight of his love for his son, he's so caught up in his pride over him."

"Oh, Mrs. Lawrence," Kim said, searching for words that could express her sympathy and support. "You said you wished Chan had a normal life — can't you insist that he go to college?"

"I guess I was hoping he'd want that sort of thing for himself. That's why I was so pleased when he took up with you, dear — a nice girl from outside the tennis circle. I thought perhaps finally his horizons would widen. But it seems you were only — " She stopped abruptly, her eyes wide with dismay. "I'm so sorry. I didn't mean to. . . ."

"That's okay, Mrs. Lawrence. I know, I'm just another tennis groupie to Chan. I guess he liked me because I was normal too, but that appealed to him not for what it's really worth but just for its image." Kim sighed. She'd forgotten to order lunch and now it was too late if she wanted to watch the women's finals before Chan played.

Mrs. Lawrence saw her glance at her watch.

"You go ahead, dear," she said, picking up a fork and toying with the untouched salad before her.

Their eyes met and Kim saw appreciation there.

"It's meant so much to talk to you." Mrs. Lawrence managed a smile. "I think — I think perhaps I can bring myself to talk to my son and my husband."

"I *know* you can," said Kim sincerely. She felt she'd learned something, too, about Chan and her lightning relationship with him. But maybe it was something she'd known, deep inside, all along.

The men's finals of the Newport Invitational Tennis Tournament seemed to be over almost before they began. But that might have been, Kim thought wryly, because she felt she'd seen it all before.

In the third set, with the score one-all, Chan blew his cool. He called the linesman an idiot. The umpire warned him against such an outburst.

When he disputed another call at the top of his lungs, the umpire fined him one point.

"Your next penalty, Mr. Lawrence, will be the loss of one game," said the umpire.

A group of girls sitting near Kim began to clap and chant. "You tell 'em, Chan. Do your McEnroe act!"

Kim almost laughed, remembering Chan's "McEnroe and Tatum" remark and how she'd fallen for it so heavily.

Chan lost a long, dramatic rally; he threw his racket in sheer exasperation. He forfeited a game.

That seemed to be what he needed to get his act together. He attacked ferociously. He won the match.

Kim was limp. It was finally over.

Chan accepted the trophy triumphantly. The cheers and whistles of his groupies were deafening. He grinned and waved to them, to the cameras, to Kim. Mr. Lawrence, an iron grip on Kim's wrist, bucked the departing crowds to join him on the court.

Kim found herself facing a TV camera once again. But this time was different. She stood apart from Chan and let Mr. Lawrence take center stage instead. She couldn't have cared less about being on the eleven o'clock news. All she wanted now was to be back with *real* people, where she belonged.

Chapter 17

It was a relief to be back at the Albatross — more than a relief, it was a joy. I love you, wonderful bookstore, she thought. "I love you, wonderful parents!" she said out loud.

She gave both her parents a big hug. She hadn't told them the whole story when she got in late the night before, but she knew her mood was communicating the gist of it to them. They would wait for the details; they respected her need for space.

"And I love you, wonderful puppy!" The surprise greeting Sasha on her return home was that not only had her mother pledged twenty dollars to the Humane Society, but she'd actually driven over there to adopt a shaggy gray puppy, newly christened Homer.

"He's already housebroken," Mrs. Jenkins said. "We turned him loose this morning while we had breakfast."

"And he had breakfast — he ate the leg of a

chair." Mr. Jenkins laughed wryly.

Mrs. Jenkins waved a hand. "I always hated that chair."

Homer also seemed to like to strip the backs from books and chew the pages.

"He's trying to read!" Sasha exclaimed with delight.

"Just keep him in the cage while he's in the store," Mrs. Jenkins advised. "Once he gets the hang of reading, not chewing, we can let him loose in here."

The phone rang. Mr. Jenkins signaled for Sasha. "We're off to the book fair, honey, and the call's for you. We'll be back by dinnertime." Mrs. Jenkins waved from the door.

"Sasha?" It was Chris. "I was worried about you yesterday. I just wanted to let you know that today's my day off from Congressman Barnes's office, if you'd like a visitor at the Albatross."

"Oh, Chris, thanks. You're a pal. I've had a lot on my mind and yeah, I'm alone here and if you want to come by I think I'm ready to talk about it."

"By the way, Sash, did you happen to see Chan Lawrence's match on TV last night?"

"No, I missed it — you'll have to tell me all about it when you come by!"

The Albatross's door bells jingled not thirty seconds later. It wasn't Chris, it was Rob.

"Hello, sweetheart!"

Sasha's heart skipped a beat. Rob wasn't talking to her, though, he was talking to the puppy. He took Homer right out of her arms. Homer was ecstatic.

"How are you?" Rob said, turning this attention from Homer to Sasha. "Did you have a nice weekend?"

Sasha blushed. "It was fine. How was *yours*?" What she really wanted to ask was: Is Cathy Silver still around?

"It was fun." Just what I was afraid of, Sasha thought.

Rob smiled enthusiastically. "I had a good time showing Cathy around Georgetown and D.C."

"Oh, yes, Cathy." Sasha couldn't bring herself to ask any further questions.

When Rob didn't say anything more about Cathy, she told herself she wouldn't care.

"What can I do for you?" That was one question that wasn't dangerous. "Need some reference material for your book?"

"Actually," Rob said slowly, "I came by to ask you if you'd collaborate with me on a story; a feature for the *Bulletin*." His eyes met hers and then he looked away quickly. Sasha was surprised to see that he'd flushed slightly under his tan.

"It would be fun to work together, I thought," he finished. He turned back to Homer and studied the puppy's floppy gray ears as if he'd never seen anything so fascinating.

Sasha felt a strange thrill somewhere between her heart and her stomach. And she knew why she felt it. It was Rob.

It was Rob, definitely. But it wasn't just his sandy blond hair and deep hazel eyes, or his strong build and that sudden smile that invited everyone around him to laugh. Although all that was thrilling enough. It was the person inside, the caring and comfortable guy Sasha found so easy to talk to and be herself with. She'd like to get to know him better; maybe it could never be a romance but that was okay.

"What's your idea for a feature, Rob?"

"Oh." He put down the dog. "I guess I'm kind of putting the cart before the horse, so to speak. I came up with the other idea first. You, I mean."

Sasha blushed. She risked a look at Rob. He was looking at her. She felt a surge of electricity in the room. Rob didn't drop this eyes. It was almost as if he was trying to send her a silent message, or read her mind, or both.

Just then there was another jingle. Sasha started. It was the door. In whirled Chris, looking as fresh as the summer breeze she brought with her, in a lime green skirt and loose white blouse. To Sasha's great surprise, Kim followed practically at her heels.

"Kim!" Sasha exclaimed.

"Kim?" Chris about-faced. "Kim!"

"Kim!" Rob called out, laughing. All three girls looked at him. "It was just too much of a temptation," he explained.

"Hi, guys," Kim said. "Did you miss me?"

"Did we ever!" Chris nodded vigorously. "Our Fourth of July celebration just wasn't the same without you. Although," she added, choosing her words carefully, "we *did* get to see you on TV."

"Oh, the coverage of the tournament." She laughed, her eyes dancing slyly. "What did you think of it?"

"Well, it was certainly a thrill that Chan won."

"My friend the diplomat." Kim gave Chris a quick hug. "Thanks, Chris."

Rob had moved off to the history section — his favorite, Sasha noted — as if to give the girls a chance to talk in private.

Now Kim approached Sasha, her face suddenly serious. "Did *you* miss me, Sash?" she asked quietly. " 'Cause I missed *you*. I was hoping you were having a good time with Wes. Whenever I wasn't — having a good time — I was glad that at least one of us was doing things right."

Sasha smiled and shook her head. "Not necessarily doing things right, but doing them differently."

"What I mean is, I don't care about all that. I'm sorry, Sash. Will you forgive me?"

Sasha hugged her soundly in answer. "Kim, you're crazy. There's nothing to forgive."

"I'm glad." Kim's green eyes were warm. They crinkled in a smile. "Because I hated being mad at you."

"Me, too," said Sasha.

Chris pulled up a stool at the counter and rested her chin on her hand. "About that match, Kim . . . you had a good time with Chan?"

Kim tilted her head to one side and considered.

"Yes, I had a good time. It was certainly a *learning* experience."

Sasha's curiosity was piqued. Kim was being very mysterious about Chan and her whole weekend. She might have guessed that things were going well between them because Kim was in such good spirits, or she might have guessed the opposite for the same reason. What confusion!

"Well," Kim continued to Chris, "if you enjoyed watching Chan play on TV, then you'll really be happy to hear this," she paused for effect, "winning at Newport gave him a big name. Out of the *kindness* of his heart, he's going to conduct a tennis clinic, here in Rose Hill, tomorrow. For any kids who want pointers from a famous pro. It's going to show on cable TV, Mr. Bennington's station. *And* he's going to make a pitch for the animal shelter." Kim waited for their reactions.

Sasha eyed Kim suspiciously. Her words had been those of a devoted fan and girl friend, but she had most definitely rolled her eyes when she uttered the word *kindness*.

Suddenly she knew everything was all right with Kim. She wanted to giggle. But Kim had something up her sleeve; she'd let her tell them in her own way.

Chris was still trying to be tactful. "Think of all that publicity," she said kindly.

"Yeah, for Chan," Sasha couldn't resist adding. But Kim didn't rise to it. Her expression remained serene.

Chris met Sasha's eyes and they both shrugged.

Kim looked at her watch. "Oops! I've got to run. Earthly Delights needs me — I have three carrot cakes to bake."

She sprinted for the door, tossing a bright smile over her shoulder. "I'll see you at the tennis clinic tomorrow, okay? And spread the word to the gang, I want *everyone* to come!"

"Well, Hurricane Barrie's back in town," Chris

said, shaking her head with a laugh. "I think everyone's still reeling from the switch she pulled with Woody and Chan. And I *won't* pretend to *like* him, but I love her too much to hold it against her." Chris pushed back a strand of blond hair with a sigh. "Poor Woody," she said.

"I wouldn't be too sure about that, said Sasha. "No," she repeated slowly, "don't count Woody out yet."

Rob lifted a hand in good-bye from the other end of the store. "I'm off — inspiration strikes, and I'd better get back to my typewriter before the moment passes. Give my regards to your folks, Sasha. And I'll be back tomorrow — Maybe we can talk about the feature."

Chris watched him go. "He's a really nice guy," she commented.

"He is."

"Oh, Sasha," Chris was looking at her watch. "We blew it — we can't have our talk. My mom needs the car in five minutes! How about tonight? Do you want to come over and rent a movie with me and Brenda?"

"I'm having dinner with Wes," Sasha said. "My story will keep until tomorrow."

"I'll see you at the clinic then." Chris pulled a face.

"Bye. Talk to you later."

The door closed behind Chris with a jingle. Sasha went to the paperback fiction stacks and pulled out her Edith Wharton book. She pulled the stool behind the cash register and sat down to read.

Chapter
18

When Wes phoned the bookstore that afternoon and asked Sasha to have dinner with him at the Bistro Français, she agreed with a feeling of calm certainty. Tonight, she promised herself, she was going to tell him that she wanted to break up. She had to express her own feelings, once and for all.

Deciding this made Sasha feel free. She moved around her room lightly as she got dressed for dinner. Hearing the doorbell, Sasha took a deep breath and walked downstairs.

When she opened her door, Wes held out his arms to her and swept her into his strong embrace. Feeling his familiar cheek against her hair, Sasha fought back her tears and said in a low voice, "Can we . . . take a walk to the park tonight before we go?"

"Wes," she said tentatively when they got to a winding, solitary street nearby, "I have to talk to you. . . . It's hard to explain this, because, well, you're the only guy I've ever loved. . . ." Her voice trailed off and Wes turned his eyes away from her. "It's just that — something's changed between us, and I — I'm not sure we belong together anymore."

His arm was around her shoulders but it was very heavy and still. Suddenly Sasha realized that Wes would never hold her again the way he had the night they first kissed.

"Could you take me home, Wes?" she asked softly.

He nodded. Neither one moved. They both turned to look at the other at the same time.

"Oh, Sasha — "

Suddenly their arms were wrapped around each other. But it was a sense of sadness and loss they were grasping, not one of passion.

Wes rocked Sasha as she cried. "You were right, the other night in the boat. It's not working. I wanted it to so badly, I wanted you to be the perfect Navy girl friend, but you're not." He buried his face in her hair. "You're so beautiful. You're Sasha. But Sasha could never change into the girl I was imagining by my side at Annapolis."

"It's not fair." Sasha looked at him, her eyes bright with tears. "It's not fair for people to fall in love who aren't right for each other."

"We did fall in love, didn't we?" Wes's green eyes glowed down at her with love and understanding. For all the times Sasha had been frustrated by the gulf between them, now in this last bittersweet moment she somehow felt closer to him than ever before.

Sasha rested in his arms and a painful, peaceful silence washed over her. Wes was stroking her hair.

"Tomorrow is my appointment for my solo flight at the Aviation School, Sasha — the final requirement for my private pilot's license. . . . I wish it could have worked for us, Sasha, but the Navy — well it's my life."

Sasha sighed, her throat aching. Wes took her hand.

"Come on. I'll take you home."

Kim arrived early the next morning at the Kennedy High School tennis courts, where the televised clinic was to be held. She parked her bike and freed her tennis racket from the strap behind the seat. She stretched her arms over her head and her yellow-and-white-striped T-shirt slipped up over her belly button.

Oh, I feel so *good*! she thought as she tramped across the lawn just west of the school. There's something to be said, she thought smiling ruefully to herself, for making a big mistake, because then you get the big satisfaction of admitting you were wrong.

And now she was going to admit it to the whole world, or rather to her friends, and they were all that mattered anyway. They'd get to see Chan — the real Chan — in action at the clinic, and Kim was sure he'd be in his usual splendidly selfish form. They'd get to see *Kim* see the real Chan, too, someone she'd been completely blind to up until — could it only have been four days ago?

Only one thing was wrong in Kim's world

this morning. Only one thing, but it was the biggest thing of all. It was a cloud big enough to fill the whole sky and make her forget the sun was shining.

Woody Webster. How could she have let him get away from her? The sweetest, kindest, funniest guy she'd ever met, and he'd been *hers* until she'd made a fool of herself over Chan Lawrence. Kim swiped at the gleaming lawn with her racket and the drops flew, catching the sunlight like tiny round rainbows. Maybe he'd be at the clinic. Kim's spirits perked up again. If only she had a chance to apologize, she'd find a way to make it up to him.

The area around the tree-shaded tennis courts was already bustling. She scanned the crowd for Chan. She had told him she'd be happy to help out, she was even thinking of posing as a student in his class. It wasn't so much that they were on bad terms now that things hadn't worked out between them; Chan's interest in her had simply melted like an ice cube on a hot sidewalk.

Kim spotted Phoebe, Sasha, Ted, Chris, Brenda, and Brad — no Woody — and hurried to join them. A big TV truck with the Bennington Cable logo on the side was parked on the grass next to the courts. A director of some sort talked to a dozen kids around twelve years old.

Kim really didn't know what was going to happen next; she was as curious as the others. When everything was set, Chan Lawrence appeared as if by magic. Kim walked over to him. "Just tell me what you want me to do," she said politely, glancing over her shoulder to make sure

Sasha and the others were watching.

Chan looked right through her. "Look, it's all taken care of," he said. "The best thing you can do is just hang out on the sidelines. Make like you're part of the onlookers."

Kim backed off with a shrug and a wide grin at the gang. "What can I say?" she said when she rejoined them. "This is obviously a *very professional* session." Just keep your eyes on the very professional idiot, she thought.

Chan showed the kids the various grips and basic strokes. He had them swing their rackets — forehand, backhand, two-handed backhand. And all the time he smiled and joked, the epitome of helpfulness and generosity.

So far, though, Chan hadn't attempted to mention the animal shelter. He still hadn't mentioned it when he walked off the court to stand beside a gorgeous, brand-new car, only slightly brighter than his tennis whites. There was a girl behind the wheel — Laurie Bennington.

The camera was on them. Chan faced it and flashed his killer smile. "If you want to know the choice of tennis champions. . . ." He did a pitch for the car company and patted the car.

"This one's mine." He grinned broadly and waved for Laurie to move over so he could jump into the driver's seat. "You can get your own at your local car dealer."

Then he winked. "You'll have to find your own girl, though. This one's mine."

He leaned over, kissed Laurie, and pulled the car away from the court. Laurie waved gaily at the camera as they sped away.

"He never mentioned the animals!" Brenda was outraged. "He was doing a commercial! And I bet they *gave* him that car."

Brad stood open-mouthed.

"Trust Laurie," Ted hooted. "I have to give that girl credit: She has a nose for an opportunity. Poor Dick's going to come back from the shore and see his girl friend's face on every billboard in town. The new queen of commercials."

Sasha and Kim had fallen to the grass helpless with laughter. Now Kim sat up, still giggling.

"I'm sorry, Kim," Phoebe said.

"I don't know what to say." Chris looked concerned.

"The guy's a jerk, that's all there is to it," said Ted. Chris elbowed him in the ribs.

"Ted's right." Kim stood up and brushed a few pieces of grass off her yellow shorts. She smiled. "I'll tell you what you can say, you guys, to make me feel better. Tell me I'm a jerk too, but that you feel sorry for me and want to buy me a pizza for lunch."

There were a few cheers. Of course someone said, "You're a jerk, Kim!" But Kim couldn't have been happier. She was back where she belonged, she was *herself* again. Even though she was going to be awfully lonely without Woody.

One of the tires on Sasha's bike blew out while she was pedaling to the Albatross from the tennis clinic. Sasha giggled as she bent over to inspect the damage; she pictured Laurie and Chan posing in the car for the camera. What a stunt.

She was so glad things had worked out for Kim,

or rather not worked out. Sasha knew she and Kim both felt a lot alike; very relieved and more than a little bit sad. But maybe Kim could patch things up with Woody; if Sasha knew Woody, and she thought she did, he wouldn't let Kim be lonely for long.

She, however, would never patch things up with Wes. That was over, forever. And as for Rob Kendall, it had only been her imagination that he could possibly care for her.

The rear tire was cleanly split. There was nothing for it; she'd have to walk her bike the rest of the way. Sasha wiped her hands on her pink-and-gray-striped shorts. Just then, a black Renault Alliance pulled up beside her.

"Need a hand?" Rob Kendall asked, his left cheek dimpling in a friendly smile.

Sasha blinked. It was really Rob. "Do I ever," she said gratefully as he heaved her bike up and into the trunk of his car. He held the passenger seat door for her.

"To the bookstore, I presume?"

"You bet."

Rob drove at a leisurely pace toward town. This *is* a moment to savor, thought Sasha, drinking deeply of the summer scents that breezed in the open window. Summer won't stay around forever — you've got to make it last. And Rob won't stay around forever, either, Sasha thought with a secret sigh. In September he'd go back to St. John's.

Sasha turned to him with a smile. "Do you think you'll finish that novel by the time you have to start school again?"

Rob laughed. "That's a good question. I really don't know. I was talking about that just the other day with my roommate Bill's girl friend Cathy — "

"*Whose* girl friend Cathy?" Sasha's heart stopped. If she'd been driving, she would definitely have clipped a few mailboxes.

Rob glanced at her in surprise. "My college roommate Bill — his girl friend Cathy was staying at the Petersons' with me last weekend while she did some last minute summer job hunting in Washington. You met her — remember?"

Sasha was laughing helplessly for the second time that morning. She slapped her hand to her forehead.

"What's the joke?" Sasha's laughter was infectious and Rob was grinning, even though he didn't know why.

"Oh, nothing." Sasha shook her head and swallowed another round of giggles. "You just made my day, that's all."

"I — you don't mean — Sasha, you didn't think Cathy was my — " Rob stopped the car in front of the Albatross and looked at her in amazement.

Sasha met his eyes. She suddenly felt shy. Something was out in the open now between them and while it felt right, it made things different.

It made things better. Because Sasha didn't feel shy for long. Rob didn't let her. He threw his head back and howled with laughter. That started her up again. The two of them laughed until they were weak.

Sasha dabbed at her eyes. Laughing had

squeezed a few tears from them, the last ones left over, she imagined, from her breakup with Wes. Now all the tears were out, thanks to Rob.

Rob put his hand under her chin and turned her face to his. "Does this mean what I think it means?" he asked seriously.

"I'm not sure," Sasha answered. "What would that be?"

He grinned. "That you wouldn't mind if I started hanging out at the Albatross, perhaps even a little more frequently than I've been doing. That you'll work on that feature with me, if I come up with a subject for it, maybe even if I don't."

"I wouldn't mind," said Sasha sincerely.

Rob leaned across her and flipped open her door. "Then go on — get to work. I'll see you later."

Sasha hesitated for a second, feeling a little bit deflated. She'd hoped they'd say good-bye with a kiss.

Rob looked at her and laughed. "I know what you're thinking, Sasha."

She blushed.

"You're just going to have to wait. I want to do up our first date in style."

Sasha looked into his warm hazel eyes and smiled. She hopped out of the car and pulled her bike out of the trunk.

"Good luck with the book you're writing."

"I'll be back for your opinion on it."

Sasha wheeled the bike up the sidewalk to the Albatross. "I love you, world!" she sang.

Chapter *19*

Kim biked back to her house with a heavy heart. She was relieved to be rid of Chan once and for all and to know her friends hadn't written her off for lost. But nothing could console her for the one thing she'd done that was worse than anything else.

For hurting Woody.

Kim skidded into her driveway and dropped her bike on the front lawn. She picked up the copy of the *Rose Hill Bulletin* that had been tossed there and went into the kitchen. No one was home.

She threw the *Bulletin* down on the table. It flipped open. There was a note clipped on the front page.

Her own name caught her eye. It was a handwritten note that read: *Kim, please check the second page of the Lifestyles section.*

She had a sinking feeling. It was probably a

big story about Chan's tennis clinic. She didn't want to see it, but curiosity got the better of her.

Kim stared at page two and nothing happened. Then it popped right off the page at her. The Pet of the Week picture, ready to be adopted. Call the Humane Society.

She did a double-take. The picture showed a crazy, long legged dog. Sitting on the branch of a tree. Kim burst out laughing.

The caption under the picture said: *Unusual pet. Wonderful disposition. Loves children. Marvelous, devoted companion. Lots of love to offer. For adoption, please call.* . . . It was Woody's number.

The doorbell rang. She jumped, her heart in her throat. She tiptoed to the front door and peered nervously, hopefully through the glass.

It was Woody. In the flesh or, more accurately, in the fur. He was wearing the dog outfit and when he saw her surprised face in the window he even managed to wag his tail.

Kim laughed and whipped open the door. Next thing she knew she was caught up in a furry embrace.

"Oh Woody, you nut!" Kim exclaimed, tears sparkling in her eyes. "Get in the house right now, and get *out* of that crazy costume."

Woody unzipped the shaggy dog suit and let it fall to the ground. He kicked it aside with a grunt. And he was her Woody again, curly hair, red suspenders, and all. She wouldn't trade a thing. Kim put out her arms and Woody drew her close.

After a long moment, he held her away from

him. He looked at her and his eyes were shining with love, but also with doubt.

"I'm back, Woody," Kim said softly, feeling more than a little ashamed of herself for being the cause of that doubt.

"Are you?" he asked quietly.

"I'm here, aren't I? *You're* here. Oh, Woody!" She blinked at the tears in her eyes and paused to take a deep breath. Then the words started coming out so fast she didn't know what to do with them. "It was all wrong being with Chan, it was all a horrible mistake. I never stopped loving you, Woody, even when I was in the hotel in Newport, and especially when Chan threw his racquet. I'm back and all I want is to be with you. I thought you'd never take me back. Please say you will!"

Kim threw her arms around Woody's neck.

"Whoa, girl! What a tackle! Ted could use you to back him up on the football team." He grabbed Kim's wrists and brought her arms back around to the front.

"I just want to understand something before I let you wrap me around your finger again. No — " he held up a scolding finger when Kim leaned forward to give him a kiss, " — none of that, Kimberley." He was teasing her, but she heard the underlying note of seriousness in his voice. "If I let you kiss me I'll never get this said."

"I'm back," Kim repeated, her green eyes honest and caring. "I'll never leave you again."

"But that's just it," Woody said. "Why did you go away? Why did you fall for Chan?"

Kim turned and walked toward the living room

window. She needed a minute to answer; for some reason her heart wasn't cooperating with her brain. Why *did* I? she asked herself. Think.

"Something's wrong with me." Woody's voice was dead. "I'm not good enough for you. I know that."

"No, Woody." Kim spun on her heel to face him. "You are one of the best, most wonderful people I know. Don't *ever* undersell yourself that way. You're worth more than ten Chan Lawrences, and you're worth more than — well, maybe three of me." Her voice had been fierce but now she smiled.

"Then what is it Chan's got that I don't?" Woody wondered. "No — don't answer that." His laugh was forced. "Two tennis courts, a swimming pool, a Mercedes."

"Don't say it," Kim said, covering her ears. "Because I think that was all part of what I found attractive in Chan, and I'm not proud of it."

Kim tipped her head to one side, remembering. Woody was silent. "Woody, sometimes life seems ordinary, even if you're sharing it with the best of friends — and boyfriends. What I saw in Chan was a whole new world I couldn't wait to reach out and touch, once I caught a glimpse of it. But when I got it in my hands, when I was living the life of the rich and famous in Newport, I realized there was nothing there, my hands were empty."

"But you fell in love with Chan," Woody said, his voice cracking with pain. "It could happen again, you could meet someone new."

"It'll never happen like *that* again. Never. I learned my lesson. I learned the difference between falling in love with a person — " Kim put her arms around Woody's neck and this time he didn't hold her off, " — and falling in love with a glamorous image."

Kim snuggled her head against Woody's chest right under his chin. "And you know what else I learned, Woody Webster?"

"What?" He kissed the top of her head.

"I am *really* in love with you. How do you like that?"

He pretended to consider. Kim punched him lightly. "I like it, I like it," he assured her. "I *love* it."

Woody kissed her and Kim finally knew she was home. She'd strayed a long way, looking for love, to realize that she'd had the very best love right in her own backyard all along.

Suddenly she started. "The ad in the *Bulletin*!"

"What about it?"

"Half the girls in Rose Hill will be calling your number, you sly devil you!"

Woody laughed. "No danger. I'll leave a message on my machine, saying the dog's taken."

"Correction," Kim said with her heart in her eyes. "He's no dog, he's my guy."

"I love you, Kim," he said softly.

"I love you too, Woody."

Coming Soon . . .
Couples Special Edition
SUMMER HEAT!

A car door slammed and Phoebe scrambled to her feet. She pushed her thick red hair out of her eyes and peered into the dusk beyond the circle of light cast by her mother's old paper lanterns. A tall figure started up the grass toward her. "Michael! You're here," Phoebe shouted, "just like you promised." She whopped and ran barefoot across the lawn straight into Michael Rifkin's arms.

"I missed you so much, Michael!" she cried, standing on tiptoe to plant a welcoming kiss on his cheek.

"Me, too!" he said, hugging her tightly and bending his head toward hers. Before Phoebe knew what was happening, Michael's lips met hers in the dark and his greeting turned into a long kiss. For a dazzling moment she responded with her whole self. In the next second her body tensed. She turned her head away in confusion and curled her toes in the dirt.

"Rifkin — " Peter Lacey yelled from across the yard. Michael's hands abruptly fell from Phoebe's shoulders and she quickly stepped away from his side as Peter approached. "The barbecue started at four. I mean I've heard of late entrances. You've practically missed all the food!" Peter affectionately whacked Michael on the back.

Phoebe watched Michael as he began talking to Peter. His back was turned toward her and he was gesturing as he talked. Every so often he'd run his fingers through his tangled dark hair. Phoebe had a crazy impulse to run up to him, throw her arms around his neck and kiss him — right in front of everyone. But she couldn't. No matter how lonely she felt, she was afraid of falling in love again. So she hugged her arms to herself and kicked forlornly at a clump of dandelions, trying to stop the quivering in the pit of her stomach. But the more she watched Michael, the more quivery she felt. And then she had another very scary feeling — as scary as falling in love: How much longer would a great looking, incredibly popular guy like Michael Rifkin be available? If she could ever face love again, would he still be there waiting for her?

Suddenly Phoebe saw as clear as day that Michael had been biding his time for three whole months now, waiting patiently for her broken heart to heal. Ever since May he had been so careful not to touch her — not that way. Phoebe closed her eyes. In spite of the August heat, she shivered. Michael had waited long enough, and in her heart Phoebe knew their kiss hadn't been a mistake.